SCORPION SWARM

MICHAEL COLE

SEVERED PRESS
HOBART TASMANIA

SCORPION SWARM

CHAPTER 1

He saw smoke rising from the engine.

John Rey closed his eyes and opened them again. He was on his back, roughly fifteen feet from the overturned Dodge pickup truck. He didn't even remember hitting the ground. He just remembered the black, jointed shapes emerging from between the thick rows of green island ferns. Then there was the impact. That huge, sudden impact...

It was supposed to be a routine trip, like his team had performed every few weeks under the supervision of Vergil. It was a simple assignment: go to the ridge and discard the failed lab remains. Their Leader and his Second-in-Command would manage the facility and the hostages they kept. John Rey thought he had been blessed with a sunny morning. Golden rays illuminated the road, paved several weeks ago by their construction team. But that sunlight shined down on more than dirt road and island flora. They had seen the black pits, burrowed deep into the earth. They hadn't been to the ridge in two, maybe three weeks, but John Rey knew those pits were not there before. Even Vergil took notice of them, and he wasn't the type to pay attention to inconsequential things such as holes in dirt.

What worried them more was there was no sign of the patrols. There were supposed to be men all over the island. Every time John Rey left the facility on an assignment, he ALWAYS passed one of the patrols. But today, they saw nobody in passing. They saw no animals either. Usually they would have to shoot a deer or warthog that would get in their way. But today, the island offered them no friendly company.

Then they got to the chasm.

The ambush was sudden. The team was not aware of the danger until two of their comrades had been taken. It was as though they were being ambushed by evil spirits.

Then he saw them. They were not spirits, though to him, they may as well have been. They were demonic enough; Enormous creatures that

1

up until now only existed in his nightmares. They attacked with a series of snapping claws and lashing tails, dripping a soupy substance from the barbed tip.

Per Vergil's command, John Rey boarded the bed of the truck with another of his comrades and provided cover fire with his AKM. They were relentless. They chased them relentlessly, with no sense of fear. They were locked on, like a homing missile to a target.

Then came the drumming. The earth shook beneath the wheels of their truck, jittering the vehicle as it sped. All John Rey saw was the black shell and the flickering appendages. The impact was hard and sudden. The vehicle flipped and he was airborne.

The truck lay on its left side, teetering slightly toward him. Its engine clunked and sputtered. He could see the passenger wheels up in the air. They were still spinning, slowly coming to a stop. He had only been out for a minute at most. He remembered the army of creatures that chased them. Adrenaline soared through his veins, clearing his fuzzy vision. He looked down the road. He couldn't see past the bend, which was roughly a hundred feet down. However, he could hear those dreadful hisses. He scrambled to his feet and turned around in search of his rifle. It had been flung from his hands when the truck flipped. Where it landed, he had no idea.

He felt a tightening of a grab along his shoulder. John Rey yelped and spun back, ready to draw his knife.

"Steady yourself!" Vergil shouted, blocking John Rey's draw by pinning his wrist. He instantly recognized his Commander's rugged face. Blood trickled between the hairs of his thin brown beard and spilled onto his tactical vest. The crash had busted the windshield and cut his face. But Vergil had greater concerns than cuts and bruises.

"Where's your rifle?"

John Rey shook his head. "Lost it in the crash." He looked up past the truck. The echoes of feet drumming against the earth vibrated between the trees. Those "things" were still out there.

Vergil shouldered his rifle and pressed into the jungle. He reached the tree line and glanced over his shoulder back at John Rey.

"You coming? Or would you rather wait here and personally greet those things before they disembowel you?"

John Rey pulled his Glock 19 and started following Vergil into the jungle. He glanced about, confused and still slightly disoriented.

"Where is Jerome? And Daniel?"

Vergil waited until they entered the jungle to answer. He swept the forest with the muzzle of his rifle, looking for movement of any kind. So far, there was nothing but bright green forest and golden sun. He pressed further in.

He spoke in a whisper. "Only the *one* attacked." John Rey shuddered, thinking of the wall of black that struck the truck. "It busted right through the windshield and got Daniel and took him into the jungle. It didn't wait for me. I crawled through the windshield and saw Jerome running this way like a coward."

John Rey brushed the elongated leaves of bush leaves from his face as they pressed further in. With guns pointed, they weaved between the trees and other obstacles the island had to offer. Each step was taken with caution. John Rey nervously watched the thick bushes, worried about what may be waiting behind them.

"Sir, if I may be so bold…"

"Spit it out," Vergil snapped.

"Our visibility is drastically affected out here. Would it not be safer to follow the road? It's open, and we can see them coming…"

"Did you not see what you were aiming at?" Vergil said. "They were able to keep up with the truck. Clearly, they're faster than us on foot. We'll never outrun them. In the jungle, an obstacle for us is an obstacle for them."

John Rey didn't argue. If Vergil thought this plan was best, then it was best.

Several loud hisses pierced the air. The guerillas turned on their heels and pointed their guns toward the road. There was too much terrain in the way for them to see, but they could hear the scurrying of arachnid legs scraping the dirt road.

John Rey backed up. The Commander was right. Following the road was no option.

Loud cracks popped in the distance. Rifle shots. Behind them.

Both men turned back around. Several more shots rang out, all in three-round bursts.

"Jerome!" Vergil said. They couldn't see him. From the echo of the shots, he had to be a couple of hundred meters ahead. The two men sprinted at full speed. There was a brief pause in the shooting that lasted five seconds, then it started up again. Jerome had reloaded…no…these were different. Single shots, slightly shallower. He had switched to his pistol.

Thick leaves struck his face as John Rey followed Vergil through the jungle. He tucked his chin down and absorbed the blow from a branch with his forehead, scraping his scalp as he passed under it. He looked up, only to see another in his way. He sidestepped to avoid it, turning his gaze to the left.

3

He paused, seeing the anomaly in the side of a small hill.

"What the...?" It was another of those strange tunnels. Its oval-shaped entrance was six feet wide. It was deep. The edges were marred with a strange saliva substance.

The crack of another gunshot focused him to his task. He turned around, immediately noticing Vergil's displeasured gaze.

"You through sightseeing?"

Another series of gunshots echoed through the jungle. These were much closer. There was another shot, this one even closer. Running feet pounded the ground accompanied with the sounds of labored breathing.

The leaves of two thick bushes folded away like theater curtains as Jerome burst through them. Blood fell freely from the tears in his shirt. His face was discolored, his mouth foaming. His run reduced to a drunken stumble.

"Jerome! Where are they?" Vergil barked. Jerome stumbled, overcoming the sluggishness that was overtaking him. He tried to speak, but his words were a jumbled mess. Vergil pointed his rifle, seeing the puncture wound in his comrade's side.

Then the hisses came, and with it, the rustling of leaves. They could see the black shape rising high on its legs behind Jerome. Its tail coiled and tilted back like the hammer of a revolver. Then, as if a trigger had been pulled, it sprang forward. The curved barb hit Jerome in the back, arching him backward. Pincers, black as hell, closed down over his shoulders. Jerome disappeared in a jolting motion, immediately disappearing beyond the jungle.

Vergil discharged the weapon. A spray of bullets tore through leaves before embedding in scattered locations in the terrain ahead. He ejected the empty mag and snatched a fresh one from his vest. He reloaded and faced John Rey.

"Double back! We need to—"

John Rey's eyes were wide with fright. He pointed his pistol upward and fired, bringing the Commander's orders to a halt.

"Look out!" he shouted. Vergil glanced up and around. When he saw it, he realized his logic of retreating through the forest was flawed. What was an obstacle for them was an asset to those beasts. The creature was perched high in the tree, its spider-like legs coiled underneath. It leapt with a tremendous arch, claws drawn back and ready to snap like scissors. Vergil pointed his rifle but it was too late. It landed atop of him, driving him onto his back. He yelled, spitting blood from lungs impaled by busted ribs. Then came its tail. It arched over its head, dripping the syrupy substance from the tip of its barb.

John Rey fired with shaky hands until he emptied the magazine. He wasn't sure if he even hit the thing. The barb had sunk deep into the Commander's shoulder. Vergil struggled for several seconds, spitting blood mixed with a white foam. Soon, his movements were rigid, as though he was hit with a taser. A moment later, he was limp on his back, staring blankly at the sky. Vergil was gone.

John Rey frantically tried to press a fresh magazine into his pistol. Giving in to panic, he turned around to run.

In the chaos, he had already forgotten about the oval-shaped tunnel. He didn't even complete the first step before the black shape sprang from its entrance. John Rey screamed while squeezing the trigger of his empty pistol.

Razor-edged pincers clamped down on both arms. The creature raised high on its legs and twisted his body, wrestling him to the ground. The sting of its tail brought the struggle to its conclusion. It took a few seconds for the venom to take effect. Like a dying battery, the soldier felt the strength leaving his body. Then came pain in the form of extreme muscle stiffness.

He waited, praying for eternal sleep to take him. But it never came. He was looking up at the sky. He tried to blink but couldn't. He tried to move but couldn't. He tried to talk. He tried anything and everything but did nothing. All he could do was think, see, hear, and feel.

And the feelings came in the form of pain. The stinger lifted free from where it impaled his chest. There was the sound of it stepping around. Its shadow covered his face. Then he felt tightness as the claws gripped his shoulders. Then there was movement. His back slid along the ground, grinding dirt and grass underneath him.

He watched the canopy seemingly passing overhead. That canopy disappeared from view, blocked by the dark edge of the tunnel. Then there was darkness, and the feeling of dirt and wetness against his back as he was dragged deep into the lair.

CHAPTER 2

The man in black stared at him.

In his twenty years of being a private contractor, Rob Cashen had been approached by thousands of clients. More often than not, it was always a man dressed in black.

In this case, the man in black simply went by the name of Jayson. It was a common Filipino name, and Rob doubted that was really his. Nor did he care. He wasn't here to make friends. Jayson was an average-sized figure, a couple inches shorter than Rob's six-foot height. It wasn't often that the client representative tagged along this far into the mission. Then again, it made sense. That was the case with dealing with government entities, they always wanted to make sure the work was getting done right.

"The payment has been processed," Jayson said to Rob. He held up the screen of his iPhone, revealing bank numbers and a seven-figure dollar amount. "The remainder will be transferred to your offshore account upon completion of the task."

"It will be done," Rob said. He spoke with pleasure. This was a job he would happily do for free. The money was an added bonus. He tightened his parachute harness over his tactical gear and clipped it together.

"Ten minutes to drop-off!" the Captain announced from the cockpit.

"I'll leave you to it," the man called Jayson said. "When you eliminate the threat, you can contact us with this." He gestured to another man dressed in a Philippine Military outfit. The soldier extended his hand, holding a large satellite phone. "Nobody can track this signal. I want you to call us with this. No radio."

"Customer service is my forte," Rob said. He turned around and joined his team. They had gathered near the ramp door of the C-130 Hercules. A bunch of adrenaline junkies, they were all eager to make their dive. There was no weak link among them.

There was Muddler, whom the team praised as their mascot. Being the only female on the team had its perks. But there was more to her than her looks. She could track a termite through marshlands, light a match with a sniper round, and knock three teeth out of a dude in a bar-brawl.

Then there was Stroud, Steel, and Valentine, or as Rob referred to them: *The Three Stooges*. If more than an hour went by without them cracking immature jokes, Rob would think one of them had gone missing. But they were good fighters, all former Army Airborne. They got out of the service with the same story and desire: they were naturals at warfighting and wanted to make serious money doing it.

Standing near the back was Yellowstone, the heavy weapons and explosives expert. Rob often liked to call him the team mule. Being six-foot-seven and two-hundred-sixty pounds of lean muscle, Yellowstone often carried any heavy equipment when a vehicle wasn't handy. In this case, it was the fireworks, otherwise known as C-4 and bazookas.

Standing beside him was Myung-Dae. Only Rob could pronounce his name correctly. Everyone else knew him as Tire-man, a name acquired from his service in the North Korean military before he defected. When he wasn't ordered to point his rifle at the South, he would serve as a mechanic on trucks and heavy equipment.

Stroud held the map in a crumpled mess. Rob snatched it out of his hand and flattened it out the best he could. In the middle of the wrinkled mess was the outline of an island. Rob glanced back at the mercenary, who crossed his muscular arms over his sleeveless vest.

"It's still an improvement over your face," Rob quipped. The team erupted into laughter.

"Awww, nothing could improve this little baby face," Muddler elbowed Stroud in the ribs and pinched at the indentation in his right cheek, a forever reminder of a bullet he almost literally ate during his U.S.M.C. days.

"Don't get all girly on me, Muddler," Stroud said.

"Why? You still hoping to pick up Valentine?"

"Look at that! You're making him blush," Roger Steele called from across the aisle. He adjusted his ball cap and rested his hand on his machete handle. Valentine spit chewing tobacco on his boots and tapped a fist against the black heart drawn over his vest. Steele chuckled. "You call it a black heart, I just call it shit stain."

"Alright, you freaking monkeys," Yellowstone said. "Let the old man speak."

All eyes turned to Rob.

"Hey Pops, is the payment through or what?" Stroud said.

Rob snickered. At fifty-five, he was by far the oldest in the group. Of course, to all these knuckleheads in his team, anything over forty was considered old. But it was all good fun. He enjoyed the banter with his team. Their comradery was second to none, and he knew they always had each other's backs.

"Yes, the payment is through," Rob said. "Just stay alive through this mission, Stroud, and you can go back to your strip club splurge."

"Not sure if they'll invite him to the *Ladies Club*," Tire-man added. More laughter passed through the team. Rob glanced over his shoulder, noticing a disapproving glare from the man in black. Like most of them, he seemed to lack a sense of humor.

"Seven minutes to drop off," the pilot announced.

"Alright, ladies…and Muddler," Rob said. He unfolded the crinkled map, displaying the outline of the island they approached. "This is our destination. It's called Hollow Mauna, means Hollow Mountain." The team huddled together and gazed down on the destination. It was about twenty miles in diameter. Like many islands, it was oddly shaped, with a peninsula to the northwest and an increase in elevation toward its center.

"Looks like a porkchop," Yellowstone said.

"Everything looks like food to you, you powder monkey," Stroud said.

"That'd be a moldy porkchop," Steele said, pointing his finger at the green landscape.

"You all know the target," Rob continued. Just to be somewhat formal, he slapped down the picture of the target. All smiles faded from the group as they gazed at the square-jawed face of the man who had killed their teammate a year prior.

"Finally, we're gonna get that bastard, Isagana," Muddler said.

"We're gonna get him. Best part is we get to kill him," Rob said.

"And get paid to do it," Steele said.

"As we've learned from our last encounter, Isagana has built up his own private terrorist organization called the Red Cobras. Since we've killed his boss, he's now the head honcho. We're not sure how many men he has, but Filipino Intelligence believes they've got at least a hundred, and probably getting funding from an outside source."

"Iran?" Yellowstone said.

"Don't know," Rob said. "Not our concern. But what does concern us are the scientists they are holding hostage. Not sure what Isagana's up to, but knowing him, it's something sick."

"What kind of scientists?" Muddler asked. Rob glanced back to the man in black, allowing him to take the floor.

"Geneticists. Gene splicing specialists. Chemists," Jayson said, speaking with his arms crossed. "Dr. Bischoff is the head researcher here. His goal was to develop new ways to produce food in barren wastelands. What Isagana wants him for, we're not exactly sure."

"Isagana and most of his force should be in the research facility, which lies roughly eight miles inland from the dock area here." Rob pointed at a flat beach area south of the peninsula. He looked up at Muddler, Yellowstone, and Tire-man. "That's what you're gonna hit. Eliminate any boats they have. Prevent any means of escape. Meanwhile," he glanced to *The Three Stooges*, "you goofballs will parachute first with me. We're approaching from the east and hooking southward. We'll parachute down to their stronghold on the peninsula. Reports say they have construction equipment here. Probably to build a runway. There's a radio tower here as well. We'll eliminate that and keep them from calling for help. As I've said, they're probably getting funding from another source." Rob wrapped up the map and took a step back, looking at his team as a whole. "Any questions?"

The team stood silent. Finally, Steele raised his hand.

"These researchers. Any of them hot?"

Rob smirked. "Not sure. But don't worry. I'm sure Yellowstone will be obliged to tend to your sore ass."

"What the hell?" the explosives specialist said, taken aback by the sudden snipe. The group laughed as both he and Steele raised a middle finger.

"Three minutes," the pilot announced.

"You heard him. Get your gear and prepare to jump. Now." Rob's voice was serious this time. He was on what they called *business mode.* No more jokes. He secured his H&K416 and tightened the strap on his helmet before taking his stance ten feet from the ramp. Steele switched his cap for his helmet, then lined up directly behind Rob, while Stroud and Valentine stood on the other side of the aisle. Muddler and her team stepped back and awaited their jump.

The alarms beeped and two red lights spiraled. The ramp let out a screeching whine as it lowered. The wind tugged on their clothes. Muddler stood behind the first team and tucked her hair under her helmet.

Up front, Rob waited for the countdown. He sealed his glasses in one of his pouches and replaced them with his goggles. He stood ready, watching the grey-blue sky directly outside, and the blue tint of the Pacific Ocean below.

"Thirty seconds," the pilot's voice echoed in their headsets.

They could feel the C-130 Hercules turning to starboard. The military man, strapped to the side rail, approached the edge for the final countdown.

"Remember..." Jayson yelled over the wind. One of the officers gave him a headset and a mic. He placed it on, then continued, "We'll be keeping radio silence until you notify us. Keep in mind, we're not *really* here."

Rob gave a thumbs-up. *Yes, I know.* It was the same chorus he heard from every government official he contracted for. The military officer began the countdown.

"Ten, nine..."

The ramp had opened completely. Rob could see the west edge of the island, surrounded by ocean water. He leaned forward, ready to sprint.

"Five, four, three, two, one...go!"

Rob dashed over the ramp and jumped. Arms over his head, he freefell down to Hollow Mauna.

CHAPTER 3

Rob embraced the feeling of weightlessness as he descended down to Earth. Wind tugged at his outfit and gear and whished in his ear. He passed through several cloud layers, swishing the vapor into twisting shapes.

From five-thousand feet high, the island looked like a large green rock. He could see its entire outline. It matched the image on the map almost perfectly. The center was a huge mountain, covered entirely in thick jungle. Directly below him was the northwest peninsula.

The island grew larger as he closed in on it. After a minute, he could no longer see its overall shape. The fine details of the various species of trees came into view.

He needed to wait until he hit five-hundred feet before deploying his chute. Too high, and he would alert the terrorists near the construction site. He could see the tower nearly a quarter mile to his left. It stood along the tree line, overlooking a barren section of the peninsula. As their intel indicated, the Red Cobras had some construction in the works.

Rob took a moment to look up. High above him were three dots descending like meteors from the plane. It was Muddler, Yellowstone, and Tire-man had timed their jump just right and were on track for landing near the dock.

Looking down, he almost couldn't see the ocean. Below him was nothing but green canopy. It was time. So far, the jump had gone perfect. They were about a quarter-mile inland. At this range, the trees would conceal their chutes from the view of the terrorists at the construction site.

Rob pulled his cord, launching his parachute. The ripstop nylon spat out the pack and expanded, slowing his fall drastically. Rob straightened out, now floating feet-down above the trees. His three teammates pulled their chutes and gradually glided in circular motions, like vultures hovering over a carcass.

Their feet grew steadily nearer to the trees. They were thirty feet above them now. Rob braced for impact, lifting his feet to help control his descent. Their chutes would get caught up in the branches, forcing them to climb down. It was part of the plan, as stealth was a major factor in overtaking this enemy.

Suddenly a strong gust of wind swept over the peninsula, dragging their parachutes along with them.

"Shit," Rob muttered. It was like an invisible hand had grabbed hold of him. He tried to angle the parachute to redirect himself, but the winds had already launched him eastward, right toward the edge of the cliff.

It only lasted a few seconds but was enough to turn their landing into a chaotic mess. He saw Valentine snag on the top branches of a tree. Steele and Stroud were still circling behind him. Right now, all Rob could do was focus on himself. He pulled on the straps to steer himself back into the interior of the peninsula, but the momentum was too great.

The parachute spun, swinging Rob over the trees. A moment later, he realized there were no trees under him. He had passed over the canopy line and was now over a cement runway. A hundred feet beyond that was the cliff edge.

"Just my luck," he said to himself. He yanked down on the straps, angling the parachute to unlevel it. The edges tucked downward, turning the glide into a drop. He let himself fall until he was a few feet over the pavement, then leveled the parachute to control the landing. His boots touched down on the cement runway. He grabbed at the clips to detach his harness.

Just then, another draft tugged on his parachute, yanking him across the runway. Rob felt his boots skating over the cement right up to the cliff edge. He unsnapped the clip and yanked the harness free. The parachute twisted, the cords thrashing about as the wind carried it down to the water.

Free of its pull, Rob spun around and threw his arms out. Gloved fingers clawed at the rocky edge, preventing his fall. The parachute floated free behind him, twirling down to the Pacific blue. His feet dangled below him. He lifted his right boot in search of any tiny ledge or bump he could use to boost himself up. After several tries, he couldn't find anything.

Rob glanced down below. Two-hundred feet below his boots, the water crashed into jagged-shaped boulders as large as cars. Water ran over razor-sharp edges that could cut a man in two if he landed on them.

Rob felt a tightening around his wrists. He looked up, seeing Steele hunched at the ledge. He already had his cap back on over a radio headset. Four inches below it was a shit-eating grin.

"Seems like I'm always getting you out of trouble, Old Geezer," he said. He tugged back as hard as he could, pulling Rob up over the ledge. Rob stood up and took one last glance at his close call below.

"Yeah-yeah," he said. "Careful there, Junior. Time marches on for us all."

They shouldered their H&K416s and conducted a sweep of the immediate area. So far, there were no hostiles in sight. Valentine and Stroud emerged from the tree line. Armed with MP5 submachine guns, they joined Rob and Steele at the inner edge of the runway.

"Trailers are that way," Rob said, pointing south.

"You think they know we're here?" Valentine asked.

"If they did, I think we'd see their welcoming party by now," Rob answered. He watched the runway for any movement. "Can't wait too long. Muddler's group should be hitting the dock any minute now. Can't risk these guys calling in backup."

He raised his hand flat and waved it forward, signaling for the team to move out. They ducked back into the trees, keeping in the shadows as they converged on the site.

CHAPTER 4

The mercenaries branched out, moving with caution as they approached the construction site. Twenty feet in from the tree line, they crouched low and observed their attack point. To their surprise, there was no movement. There was nearly two-hundred feet of space between the cliff and the tree line. Near the trees were two trailers, both lined up parallel with the road. One was a large office model, nearly eighty feet in length. Several feet beside it was a motor-home motel, only a few feet shorter than the office model. Scattered along the incomplete runway were three cement trucks, two bulldozers, and a backhoe.

Rob kept low at the base of a tree, keeping his weapon pointed as he searched for any movement. He had a good view of the site. Surprisingly, there was nothing. This time of the day would be prime time for runway paving. He worried for a minute that Muddler, Yellowstone, and Tire-man had been seen, and that this group may have left to reinforce the dock. Then again, they didn't hear any gunfire. Knowing Muddler, she would never let herself get captured.

"Let's move," he said. "Steele, Stroud, check around the backhoe there, then disable the radio tower. Once you're done, move around to the office trailer and kill any Cobras that are inside. Val, you and I will hit the mobile home first. Go in. Eliminate any Cobras you see. As always, remember to check your targets. Remember they have hostages on this island."

"Yes, Pops," Stroud said.

With a wave of their leader's hand signal, the team moved out. Steele and Stroud moved around the backhoe, checking all sides to make sure no terrorists hid behind it. The tower was just another twenty feet down south along the tree line. Keeping an eye out for possible contacts, they hurried to the hundred-foot steel structure. At its base was a small steel box. Steele pulled his prized machete from his vest and struck the metal box with the blunt end. The metal door broke open, exposing all kinds of wires and components.

Valentine and Rob moved to the mobile home. They checked their corners and ran around the front, coming to a small set of steps that led to the entrance. Rob stopped at the front of the steps and gazed at the trailer.

"What the…?"

Jagged pieces of siding littered the ground. Several giant groves lined the front of the trailer. The walls were peeled out like flower petals, exposing insulation, wood planks, and electric wiring. It was as though someone had taken a giant pair of tweezers to the trailer.

The front door had been ripped off its frame completely and torn into several pieces. Its fragments were scattered on the ground, edges frizzled and rough, looking as though someone had run a chainsaw to it. Rob moved up the steps, seeing portions of the door still attached to the hinges. Blood and other dry fluid caked the handrails like paint.

"I've seen Texas road signs in better condition," Valentine whispered.

Rob slowly ascended the steps, keeping his muzzle fixed on the entrance. As his foot came down on the top step, he sprang inside and crouched into a firing stance. Valentine followed and hugged the corner, ready to fire.

Sunlight beamed through the various breaches, illuminating the inside of an empty trailer. Four empty beds lined the main living section, their mattresses torn to shreds. Rob lowered his rifle and looked around. Between the beds were several beer bottles laying among shards of broken glass. A breeze came in from several broken windows above the beds.

"Looks like last night's shindig got a little too wild," Valentine said.

"Keep an eye out," Rob said. He approached the opposite side of the room. Strands of blood had caked onto the walls, now a light brown color. He looked to the windows, seeing deep groves around the frame. Looking up and around, he noticed these same kinds of groves on the ceiling and walls throughout the trailer.

Equally as interesting was the rifles on the floor. The Red Cobras had a variety of armaments including AK-47s, AKMs, HKMP5 submachine guns like what Valentine had, and a couple M14 rifles.

Rob continued his sweep into the kitchen. There were several groves in the floor and wall. Looking to the right, he saw the bathroom door. At least, what was left of it. Unlike the main entrance, which had been torn out, this door was caved in, as though a bull had run smack-center into it. The mercenaries checked the remaining rooms, finding each one in a complete wreck. The floor tile was ripped up as if a jackhammer had been used. The walls were marked with bullet holes and large indentations like the bathroom door. Whatever happened, these were clear signs that numerous struggles had taken place.

Rob returned to the main room and picked up an AKM off the floor. He pulled its thirty-round magazine from its feed and emptied the bullets, counting only thirteen. He glanced back to the doorway, seeing numerous bullet holes around the frame. He then glanced to the back wall. There were several markings, but no bullet holes.

"Our friends had a visitor," Rob said.

"Whoever it was, they must've been especially eager to get these guys if they were willing to bust in half the building to get them," Valentine said.

"That's what makes it weirder," Rob said. He turned his attention to the huge breaches in the front wall. "These aren't caved in, they're caved out. Same as the door. They didn't bother blasting the hinges and kicking it in. Also..." he glanced to the back wall again, "is it just me, but does it seem that the Red Cobras were the only ones who did the shooting?"

Valentine observed his surroundings and thought about it. Rob had a point. The intruders HAD to have come in from the front, and the cobras clearly had enough time to return fire.

"Considering the number of occupants they had to overtake, you'd think there'd at least be a few bullets in the wall."

They turned around, hearing the sound of approaching footsteps. Steele came up the steps and peeked his bearded face through the doorway.

"Hey, Rob. We've secured the other trailer. And..." Steele's voice trailed off.

"And...?"

"It's a mess..." he looked around, seeing the disarray around him. "Much like this."

"Any weapons?"

"Yeah. Weapons. Bullet holes. Blood. No Cobras, though. Unless there's something we've missed, the area's clear," Steele said.

"Yeah...and we didn't have to fire a single shot," Valentine said.

"Disappointed?" Stroud asked.

"A little...yeah." Valentine massaged the black heart on his vest. Steele examined some of the weapons on the floor. Each one had been fired to some extent. He stood at the doorway, watching the crumbing streak of blood on the rail.

"What happened here? Did your pal Jayson mention any other players going after Isagana, Rob?"

Rob followed him outside. "No, but it's possible. Isagana's pissed off plenty of people. Though, unless they went the route of private contractors, they wouldn't be landing any strike teams anywhere near here without the good ol' U.S. of A. getting wind of it. We're too close to Hawaii."

"Whoa! Hey guys, check this out," Stroud called out. He pointed to a vacant bulldozer several yards up the completed portion of the runway. The frame of the cockpit had been smashed inward, as though a giant sledgehammer had been brought down on it. He hustled to the bulldozer and peered into the cockpit. The keys were still in the ignition, which was covered in blood. The leather seat was torn, the windshield shattered, and several deep grooves lined the steel along the platform.

"Hoooly shit," Valentine exclaimed.

"What the hell do you think did this?" Stroud said.

"Looks like your face," Steele remarked.

"Your sister loves it," Stroud said.

"Don't have a sister," Steele retorted. Rob ignored the banter as he studied the damage. Shattered glass crunched under his boots as he stepped onto the platform and pulled the door open. It was stuck against the ceiling which had folded down, catching its top corner. Rob gripped with both hands and tugged harder. Suddenly, the hinges busted free, nearly causing him to fall back. Rob steadied himself, then saved face by holding up the door with the pose of an action hero exhibiting superior strength.

"Yeah, nice try, Rob. Already saw the bolts sticking out of the hinges," Steele remarked.

"Eh," Rob groaned, tossing the door aside. He peered into the cockpit. Some of the blood had trickled down to the floor of the cockpit. Looking back up at the ignition, he realized the key was still turned. He reached in and twisted back into *off*, then tried starting it again. The engine groaned for a moment and died.

"Out of gas?" Valentine asked.

"Yes…" Rob's voice trailed off as he noticed the shards of glass sticking from the bottom of the windshield frame like stakes. Their edges were covered by dried blood, which had started to crumble off in flakes. He stepped out and looked behind the bulldozer, seeing the crisscrossed tracks that had been made. Whoever was driving it had it going back and forth, turning and twisting repeatedly.

Among those treads were several other markings in the ground. They were deep long grooves, always two in a row, that stretched for a few feet at a time. He glanced at the concrete, seeing the same grooves. This section of the concrete had not yet hardened completely when these marks had been made.

"Who the hell did all of this?" he asked, thinking out loud.

"I don't know, but I know this: It takes more than an anvil to crunch a bulldozer like that," Steele said.

"Any damage to the other vehicles?" Rob asked.

"Not that I could see," Stroud answered. "The backhoe appears untouched. So is the other bulldozer."

Static in their ear-pieces interrupted their thoughts.

"Team Two to Team One. How's it going up there, Pops?"

Rob adjusted the microphone on his helmet. "Just dandy. What's the status of the harbor, Tough Muddler?"

"Well...it is secured..." she said. *"Took no effort at all."*

"Care to elaborate?"

"It'll be easier if you just come down."

"On our way," Rob said. "Hang tight. We'll be there in ten."

Valentine groaned. "What are the odds they found the harbor in the same state as this place?"

"Let's get our asses down there and find out," Rob said. He hustled down the tree line, following it to a small rocky hill. Below was a quarter-mile curved path that angled down to the harbor. There was a winding roadway just wide enough for the construction vehicles to drive up. It was the most even ground they could walk on.

Rob took the lead, followed by Steele and Valentine. Stroud followed two yards behind them, watching their six to detect any surprise attacks. The sound of rustling leaves turned his attention to the tree line. Stroud turned and gazed into the trees, ready to aim and fire.

Green leaves frolicked high in the canopy as the wind brushed through the trees. He studied the branches with his eyes, looking for the outline of any snipers poised to take a shot at him.

Nothing.

Suddenly, the tall grass swayed. Stroud aimed his gun and took a couple steps into the forest, ready to engage. The grass peeled to the side, and he saw the large grey hunk moving toward him.

"Fuck!" he yelled out. He stumbled out of the jungle. He relaxed his posture and lowered his weapon. The warthog oinked and stared up at him.

"Trying to get a date?" Steele called back. The remark was followed by laughter.

Damn! Getting paranoid already, he thought to himself. The pig bobbed its head and oinked again.

"Anyone in the mood for some bacon?" he quipped. He hustled, kicking up small mounds of gravel as he caught up with the others.

"At least there's no risk of him fixing up that vegan crap. Whew! God that was a painful cookout," Valentine quipped.

"Hey! It was an honest mistake! The damn things looked the same," Stroud retorted.

"Hence, they invented labels," Rob said.

"Your mother," Stroud said. More chuckles resounded from the group as they continued down the hill.

****

The warthog watched the human as it rejoined its group and disappeared behind the rocks. It started to follow, curious to their presence, then finally returned to its routine activity of grazing. It brushed its tusks against the base of a nearby tree before proceeding to use those tusks for digging up grass and roots. It swallowed a mouthful, then proceeded to work the ground some more.

Twelve eyes watched the unsuspecting prey as it approached the dark shade twenty feet below it. Tightly clinging to the tree limb, it bent its legs at the joints and coiled its tail, ready to spring down at the right opportunity. With a simultaneous thrust from all eight legs, the arachnid dove onto the warthog.

The warthog looked up, seeing a black spider-shape drawing down. Three hundred pounds of shell crashed down on it, driving it to the ground. Razor sharp pincers clamped down on its hooves, cutting through fur and flesh. The warthog wailed and rolled, only to find itself coiled under several spider-like legs.

It squealed in agony as something sharp pierced its back repeatedly. The warthog continued to struggle, only to become increasingly sluggish. Its vision blurred and its movements slowed. After several moments, the warthog lay still in the dirt. Its brain continued firing off signals to its limbs. It tried to run away. But it couldn't.

It felt the tightness from its attacker's claws around its legs and the rubbing of dirt against its hide. The jungle passed by its eyes as it was dragged to the depths of the island.

CHAPTER 5

Muddler stared out at the ocean, watching the waves ripple from the breezes. The sky was almost equally blue, with only a few clouds to add variety. Golden streaks of sunlight soaked the beach and the trees that surrounded it.

In the middle of that tranquility was the harbor. Muddler watched the rippling waves bounce against the rusted metal of the small cargo ship. Its bow stuck out of the water nearly three hundred feet out from the dock. What was left of the dock. She looked at her watch. It had been almost ten minutes since she radioed Rob.

Several yards to the north was a gravel trail that led to the hill. She could see the cliff edge and the wall that led to the waterline. The side of the cliff was almost perfectly smooth except for the rocky shore below. Water splashed as the tide broke over the enormous rocks, a sharp contrast to the tranquil sandy beach.

She glanced to the dock and saw Tire-man strolling fifteen feet out. He couldn't go any further, despite it being a forty-foot dock. He knelt down at the broken section, seeing the spikey edges of shattered boards. Standing at the edge, Tire-man observed the rest of the dock ahead of him. There was about five feet of watery space between it and him. Several pieces had floated under the deck and bunched near one of the posts. There were other bits of deck on the dock itself, as if a huge air compressor had discharged underneath it.

Muddler kept a watchful eye on the tree line, specifically the inland trail. It was a seven-foot clearing in the forest, made specifically for vehicles. The jungle was silent. Almost too silent. She realized as she waited that there were hardly any bird calls or other animal sounds.

The crinkling of a plastic wrapper turned her attention to Yellowstone. He stood off to the side and unwrapped a power bar.

"You're eating? Already?"

"I'm bored," he said. "I tend to eat when I'm bored."

Muddler shook her head. She felt the complete opposite. She hated mysteries of all kinds. It was one of the reasons she preferred being a private contractor instead of a soldier. The jobs were straightforward: Eliminate the target, rescue the hostage, retrieve the stolen item. Payment half up front, remainder received upon completion of mission. Simple with no surprises. That was the way she liked it.

She did *not* like this. Something had gone seriously wrong on this island. The worst part was she didn't know what. She had inspected the aftermaths of hundreds of firefights, and this was nothing like them. Most of the time, judging by the position of shell casings, bullet holes, and other damage and body locations, they could figure out who was shooting at who. Though someone had clearly invaded the beach, there weren't signs of incoming fire. In fact, the only damage not caused by the Cobra's own weapons appeared to be caused by edged weapons.

Muddler turned her eyes back to the hill. She immediately recognized the rectangular glasses on her boss's face. Muddler approached the hillside and waved to Rob.

"Well shit," Steele muttered as they gazed upon the wreckage that was the harbor. Twenty yards inland from the dock was a guard shack; what was left of it. The awning had been smashed down as though a huge hammer had come down on it. The rest of the roof had been ripped to shreds. The walls on all four sides were in the same condition. Much like the trailers, the walls had been ripped outward instead of caved in.

"Looks like a paper mâché fuckup," Stroud said.

"Stop talking about your face," Yellowstone retorted.

"Okay, knock it off," Rob interrupted. He was serious. Like Muddler, he didn't like what he was seeing. He gazed at the broken dock, seeing the damage where Tire-man stood. Looking further out, he stared at the half-sunk cargo boat. He followed Muddler to the beach for a better look. He could see the edges of several breaches, most of which were near the stern. From what he could see, they were not reminiscent of artillery strikes. It almost looked as though the metal had been peeled out like an onion.

"This is weird, Rob," Muddler said. "Let me guess, you found the construction site in the same condition?"

"Yeah," he answered. "Any bodies?"

"No. Not a one. We've got weapons scattered. Some personal equipment. No people though," Muddler answered. They walked over to the shack, passing a crumbed-face Yellowstone. "If their food supply is missing, you can probably suspect this guy."

"Hey girl. Eating is the first rule of survival," Yellowstone said, spitting crumbs from his lips. With the large pack strapped to his back, he followed behind him, the submachine gun looking tiny in his enormous hands.

Rob looked at the guard shack and the various weapons scattered in the sand. He picked up an AK-47 and checked the mag. As he suspected, it was empty. However, it wasn't as though the Red Cobras had run out of ammo. Other guns were laying on the ground with fully loaded magazines. Rob peered through the broken window, immediately seeing a small armory. In that armory was the only other sign that someone had been here: human blood.

"I don't like this, man," Valentine complained. "Rob, am I right to assume that your contact didn't infer that anyone else was after the Cobras?"

"I thought you were eager to shoot people," Stroud said.

"I am. But in case you haven't noticed…" Valentine gestured out to the sunken cargo ship, "it takes more than a little posse to do that."

"Plus, we don't know *who* it is and what their agenda is," Muddler added. "They might as soon turn on us."

"Let 'em," Yellowstone muttered.

"I like your attitude, big guy," Rob said. "But for once, Val's right. I'm not keen on going forward until we've got more info. Hand me that satellite phone."

Yellowstone unloaded his pack and pulled the phone from the side pouch. Rob took it and hit the dial button.

As he walked to the side, the mercenaries kept watch. Yellowstone assembled his M60, while Stroud, Steele, and Valentine watched the trees. She looked back, noticing Tire-man was down at the dock. He was on his knees and reaching into the water.

What the hell's he up to?

He leaned up, as though giving up whatever he was up to. Then, he spun on his knees and placed his weapons on the dock, then lowered his feet into the water.

Finally, Muddler approached. She walked all the way up the dock and looked down at Tire-man, who was fully submerged. He rummaged through the weeds for several seconds, then stood up. He sucked in a breath and looked up at Muddler.

"Hey," he said.

"Am I interrupting your bath?" she said. Tire-man leaned onto the dock and smiled from her joke. She shook her head. "What were you doing?"

"I was checking out the broken planks and saw this." Tire-man extended his hand, holding a large black shard. It was as large as a pizza slice, though much thicker. At first, Muddler thought it was a piece of shell casing until she held it in her hand. If felt more like a rock. Its surface was rough and bumpy, and sandpaper-like in texture. Judging by the edges, it had broken off of something larger.

Holding it by the underside, she felt something wet and soft. She flipped the object over, seeing strands of some sort of meaty substance dangling. They were light yellow in color, likely having been faded from being in the water.

"Probably just a turtle shell," she said.

"Must be a lot of dead turtles, then," Tire-man said. He looked back down at the water. "There's about a dozen or so pieces like that."

"I don't see how it's relevant," Muddler said, tossing the shell to the side. Tire-man stepped away from the dock and ducked back down under the water. Muddler crossed her arms and shook her head, "Oh, brother. The things these guys do when they're bored…"

Tire-man reemerged, holding another piece of shell. Muddler gulped. This one was at least four times as large as the other one. The top was spiny and bumpy, with a long, arching lump running through the middle like a big rib, as though whatever it belonged to had a segmented body. Five-inch strands of meaty substance dangled from the underside.

What really caught Muddler's attention were the bullet holes. She had seen enough bullet holes to know that these had been caused by 7.62mm rounds, likely fired from one of the AK-47s. Tire-man placed the shell on the dock and dipped down a third time. He dug around in the water, pulling weeds to the side. He climbed back onto the dock, holding an empty AK-47 in his hand.

"I think it's relevant," he said.

"You might be right," she said.

Rob grew agitated as he listened to Jayson lecture him on the phone. It was the same monologue he always had to endure. It was like a math formula: 'We-pay-money-equals-you-do-job.' Rob was normally a fan of this formula until it involved digging for answers.

"*I have told you not to call unless the job was complete.*"

"I get that, Jayson, but you've given us bad intel," Rob responded. "I'm going to ask you again: Does anyone else know that Isagana and the Red Cobras are on this island?"

"*No. Not to my knowledge*," Jayson said.

"Well, by the looks of it, someone's out to get him," Rob said. "And whoever it was, they were both efficient and ruthless. Whatever trace is left can't really be tracked to anyone in particular. It's not like anything I've ever seen."

"Only one way to find out what's going on. Go and secure the laboratory," Jayson said.

"Whoever did this could still be on this island," Rob said. "I'm not keen on solving mysteries, especially when they result in my team getting massacred. We're not sure what we're dealing with, and I don't think you do either. This operation may call for a larger strike team."

"That negates the reason we hired you," Jayson said. *"We're trying to keep this quiet, not notify the States so they can send S.E.A.L.s to take care of the problem. This is an international incident our government doesn't want to deal with."* There was a brief pause. When Jayson spoke again, he softened his voice. Yet, it wasn't friendly. *"We're paying you a small fortune for a simple job. We want you to complete the task and confirm the target has been neutralized. So, I'll tell you one last time. Secure the facility. If anyone gets in your way, do what you do best. We'll take care of the cleanup."*

"And if we find nothing like we did here?" Rob asked.

"If he's not there, expand your search. If you confirm Isagana's not on the island, we'll call the mission off and pick you up."

Rob seethed in silence. It took a few moments for him to answer. "Fine," he said, finally.

"Good. And Mr. Cashen?"

"What?"

"Do NOT call again until the job's complete, or we'll see to it that that island will become your permanent residence."

"Yeah? I dare ya," Rob growled. He hung up the phone. He hated threats, and he had no qualms about calling Jayson's bluff. Jayson wouldn't sent troops or aircraft to the island without risking conflict with the U.S, so there was nothing he could do there. Should they be abandoned, Rob had contacts to get him off the island if needed, and he would happily pay Jayson a visit.

However, the easiest solution would be to conclude the deal as intended. He turned around, seeing his team standing by. Though they maintained a perimeter, there was no doubt they were listening in.

"Want to borrow this when we see that dickface again?" Steele said, pulling his machete half out of the sheath.

"Don't tempt me," Rob said. Muddler and Tire-man rejoined the group. Rob noticed the water dripping off the Korean. "Look at this guy. He's so anxious to leave he tried to swim."

"Just examining the dock," Tire-man said.

"No-go on the pickup?" Muddler asked.

"Not until we've secured the research facility," Rob said. "They're not aware of any other presence here, so stay alert."

"Eh, we'll shoot them too. And blow them up. And step on whatever's left," Yellowstone said. He raised his M60 proudly. "Lead the way boss."

Rob smirked. "Best part of being the boss is making *you* lead the way." He pointed to the gap in the jungle. "Follow the trail but don't be on it. Keep in the trees and be careful to watch for tripwires. Everyone good?" The team nodded. Yellowstone took point and guided the team into the forest. In moments, they disappeared behind the terrain. They pushed in silently, with an eight-mile journey to their target.

Once again, Muddler couldn't help but notice the silence. She looked up and around as she walked through the plants, still unable to see any sign of life. Yet, somehow, it didn't feel like they were alone on this island.

CHAPTER 6

Dr. Trevor Malloy could barely stand. Even with the crutch, he couldn't balance well on his one good leg. His leg hurt more with each passing day, and his captors would not allow access to any decent painkillers. The truth was that they wanted to keep him in pain. As Isagana had put it, pain was a motivator for getting things done.

The idea the bastard tried to plant in his head was the belief that the Red Cobras would let them go as soon as the experiment was successful. It didn't take a doctorate in Bio-Engineering and Chemistry to know that was a lie, and that Isagana had no plan in keeping them alive should they ever produce his results.

Then again, if they refused to work for him, he would have no use in keeping them alive. As much as Malloy hated these terrorists, he wasn't keen on dying. Even more important than that was making sure they didn't harm his fiancée.

Dr. Jean Kyunghee looked across the table at Trevor. He was continuously shifting his weight, trying hard not to lean too much on the crutch. She could see the hole in his pant leg where the bullet had entered. He was visibly exhausted. His eyes were glassy, he hadn't shaved in days, and his hair was a mess. The bruise on the left side of his lower jaw had darkened and she could tell that the cracked crown behind it was aggravating him as much as the leg.

"Dr. Malloy?" she said. She tried to sound as formal as possible.

He looked up. "What?" His face was wet with sweat. The distant thudding from the air conditioner was loud and annoying. Worse, it was a reminder of what these terrorists had done. They had killed Toby the maintenance man when they took over the island. The machine's jerky drumming was just another reminder of his missing presence.

"If you need to sit down, it's okay."

"Fat chance," a voice called out. Jean could see the armed men standing in the corners of the lab, watching relentlessly. They believed in cruel manipulation. Not only did they believe in it, they relished in it.

That was evident the moment they discovered she and Trevor were engaged. Since then, they repeatedly threatened to advance on her just to 'motivate' Malloy to figure out the correct gene-sequence.

"I'm fine," he said. "It's just hot in here." He returned his gaze to the supercomputer in front of him. It was wired to the artificial womb in the center of the lab. Cords and wires protruded from it, monitoring blood pressure, heart rate, and growth rate.

Jean looked up, seeing the entrance opening up. Her teacher and project supervisor, Dr. Bischoff entered the room, wearing a lab coat. A red bandana covered his bald head, having turned dark from accumulated sweat. His demeanor was calm and professional, as though it was just another day at the office. Like Jean, he understood that showing fear was the worst thing they could do in this situation.

Another man followed him, wearing a thick military vest over a camouflaged shirt. She immediately recognized Isagana's fierce stare. He was an intimidating man and he knew it. He wore fingerless gloves on his hands and always had a submachine gun strapped under his right arm. His left hand consistently rested on the handle of his knife as though eager to use it.

"Good morning, Jean," Dr. Bischoff said.

"Good morning, Doctor," she replied in a neutral tone. Bischoff noticed her glare toward Isagana and subtly shook his head, mouthing *stop*. She realized what she was doing and returned her attention to the experiment.

"Trevor, you doing okay?"

"Yes, Doctor," Trevor said. Bischoff knew he was lying. Feeling Isagana's eyes burning into the back of his skull, he decided not to press the issue. He stepped around to Trevor's left and took a look at the rippling lines on the monitor.

"Okay. Heart rate looks a little high. How's the blood pressure?"

"One-forty over ninety," Jean said. "Higher than yesterday."

"That would explain the heart rate. What about growth increase?"

"Thirty-two percent," Jean said. "Its lungs and kidneys are too small. They're at twenty-nine percent."

"Then we're on the same track as the other specimens," Bischoff said.

"It's growing too fast," Trevor said. "Its cells can't handle the fusion and the growth hormone."

"Relax," Bischoff said. He watched the numbers on the monitor. The blood pressure was gradually rising. It was now in the red. "Okay, let's go with the ACE inhibitor."

Jean moved to the back counter and filled a syringe with Enalapriat, then injected it into the IV line.

"Heart rate is rising," Trevor said.

"Body growth has increased to thirty-four percent. Internal organs are not keeping up. They're still at twenty-nine."

"What are the CV-30 levels?"

"It's overproducing," Trevor said. His voice was trembling, either from the pain or nervousness. Or both. "We're losing it. It's not…" he paused, took a breath to collect himself and leaned over to not be heard by Isagana and the guards. "This binding formula is not meant to work in animals."

"I know," Bischoff said. "Keep an eye on that heart rate." Trevor returned to his monitor and shook his head.

"It's still climbing," he said.

"Go with the anti-arrhythmic," Bischoff ordered. Jean applied the injection to the IV line. After a few moments, the heart rate started to decrease, only to pick up again. "Damn it."

"Something wrong, Doctor?" Isagana asked. Every word he spoke felt like a threat.

"Your pet's not doing very well," Bischoff said. He approached the artificial womb. It took effort not to dry-heave at the sight of the abomination in the glass tube. It had arms like an ape but had scales like a reptile. The hybrid had a large snout extending from a dome-shaped head. Clawed hands seemed to be reaching at him from bulky, muscular arms.

What haunted him most was that this was *his* creation.

The heart rate continued to increase. The creature in the womb appeared to be in some state of agony. It twisted and writhed, opening its horrific jaws as though screaming.

"Can you save it?" Isagana asked. His voice was growly.

"We're doing what we can," Bischoff said.

"Like always," Jean muttered.

"Shh." Bischoff checked the monitor on Jean's computer. The growth rate had increased by another percent, with no growth to the lungs. The heart rate continued to climb. Suddenly it slowed drastically, then flatlined. The creature inside the container stopped its movements and coiled. Bischoff looked at Isagana and shook his head. "It's gone."

"I see you've failed yet again, Doctors," the terrorist leader said.

"Well, we're not inventing new pie recipes," Bischoff said. "This is new technology. It's not easy, or else everybody would be creating genetically modified hybrids."

"Maybe. Or could it be you're not trying hard enough?"

"I assure you we are trying as hard as we can."

"Yeah, Doc? You've pulled stunts before," Isagana said. "I'm starting to wonder if you can be trusted."

"Coming from the guy who got kicked out of his own country," Jean muttered. Isagana narrowed his eyes and wrinkled his nose, then slowly approached.

"You should thank me, missy. It's only because of me that these dogs haven't set on you." Jean glanced back, seeing one of the guards licking his lips. Trevor noticed it too. He shook apprehensively, determined to jump to the defense of his fiancée. Isagana smiled. "Perhaps I've been too kind up until now. Perhaps you could use a bit of motivation to produce positive results." He winked at one of his men.

One of the guards took a step forward, his smile revealing rotting teeth. He held a submachine gun up high like a trophy, while putting his other hand near his groin.

"Wanna play, Missy?"

Trevor sprang into action, ignoring the crunching pain in his shin as he launched himself at the guard. Instruments and glass hit the floor and shattered as the table rocked.

"Trevor, don't!" Jean yelled. It was too late.

The guard turned and whipped his gun like a tennis racket, catching Trevor on the chin. He staggered back, his legs giving out behind him. He fell back against the end of the lab table. Now his thigh felt like it was about to explode. He could feel blood seeping through the bandage. His vision was a blurred mess which seemed to flash to the rhythm of his throbbing jaw.

The nerves in his head lit up as the terrorist grabbed a fistful of his hair. He pulled the doctor to his feet and smiled again. He lifted his submachine gun high, waving it in front of Trevor's face.

Bischoff shook with tension. Trevor had messed up royally and there was nothing Bischoff could do to save him. The Red Cobras had executed staff before, and for less severe reasons. One of the things he had learned was begging would only encourage their behaviors. It was a sick power fantasy, completely consistent with Isagana's ambition of creating genetically engineered super soldiers.

Isagana smiled as he watched the Cobra taunt the bio-engineer. Trevor gritted his teeth from the pain. The terrorist let go of his hand and grabbed him by the throat, then pointed the muzzle of the gun to his mouth.

"Open up and suck it," he said. "Or the lady will do the same to me." Trevor quivered and growled. "You heard me," the terrorist continued. "Open your mouth and..." He gasped as Jean flung herself over the corner of the table at him, grabbing the gun under its barrel and slamming it into his nose. The terrorist stumbled backward, shouting several obscenities in Filipino. He tapped a hand to his nose, seeing blood on his fingertips, then looked back up at Jean. She was breathing heavily, standing tense with her fists up.

"You...BITCH!" he yelled and pointed his gun.

"Alright, that's enough, Paulo!" Isagana said. The terrorist looked at Isagana, feeling betrayed.

"You saw what she did?!"

"Yeah, I saw you get your ass handed to you by a girl," Isagana said. "If you're not embarrassed now, you will be once I tell the whole squad." The terrorist kept his gun fixed on the scientist, his finger twitching inside the trigger guard.

"Isagana, I SWEAR to you, we'll get it right on the next experiment," Bischoff called out.

"Oh, you *swear*?" Isagana mocked.

"I think it's a reaction to both the gene splicing and the accelerated growth," he said. "The subjects can't seem to handle the combination. Just give us some time to go back to the drawing board and..."

"It sounds like more stalling, Doctor Bischoff," Isagana interrupted.

Bischoff sucked in a deep breath. "I promise you...it's not." Isagana stared at him with those piercing eyes. They were enough to make even the toughest of men cringe. They were like spears. Staring back at them almost made the doctor feel as though he was being lanced.

The terrorist grabbed Jean by the back of the neck and pulled her close, putting his lips to her ear. He twisted and angled themselves, making sure Dr. Malloy could see.

"One final chance," he growled. "Any more delays, I might just have to find myself some new friends. Oh, and you," he tightened his grip on Jean's neck, "anymore stunts like that, then I'll have to find another *use* for you." She felt his hot breath on the side of her head. Finally, he let go.

Jean impulsively stepped away, prompting laughter from the terrorists, including Paulo.

The laughter came to a swift end as the door swung open again. Rodrigo, Isagana's second-in-command, stepped into the lab.

"Isagana, I must speak with you," he said.

"Is it urgent?" Isagana asked.

"Yes, I believe it is," Rodrigo said.

"Fine," Isagana said. He glanced back at the doctors and pointed at Trevor. "Lock this one in the barn. It's what he gets for being so brave."

"What about this one?" Paulo pointed to Jean.

"Bring her out. Lock her in the maintenance shed."

"That place is infested with ants by now," Trevor said.

"Awww, I suppose she won't like being in there," Isagana laughed.

"Isagana, I assure you it's not necessary..." Bischoff started.

"Shut up," Jean said, silencing the doctor's plea. She glared back at Isagana. "Go ahead. Prick."

Isagana smiled then snapped his fingers at Bischoff. "You're coming too."

The group walked out the door together into the second-floor lobby. It was a cozy area, or it was, until the terrorists fouled it up. There were no cleaners available to keep the place tidy. The sofas were stained and covered in food crumbs, which stank the place especially in the humid air. The ventilation system worked periodically if the terrorist tending to it wasn't drunk. Or mechanically incompetent. But it was nothing that bothered Isagana. He had lived in far rougher conditions. If anything, this was a vacation for him.

Jean eyed the hallway at the end of the lobby, which led to the private quarters. The corridor went up and around the front of the building, containing rooms for each of the workers, or at least they used to be. As always, Jean's eyes couldn't help but glance at the bullet holes in the walls. She remembered waking up to the gunshots that had caused them. She had a fever that day and had been resting. At least the terrorists were kind enough to clean up the blood from Jesse, the intern who was working under Bischoff.

Between them and the hallway was a flight of stairs that led down to the main lobby. The group proceeded down to the first-floor. This lobby was very large and spacious, even despite the numerous offices and desks. A half-dozen Red Cobras waited, some winking at Jean as they watched her come down the steps.

"So, what's the problem, Rodrigo?" Isagana asked. Rodrigo pushed past Paulo to catch up with him.

Rodrigo was a muscular man who stood just an inch shorter than Isagana. Like his commander, he had a sharp stare, though the doctors found it slightly less intimidating when he was around Isagana. When alone, he was as ruthless as any other terrorist scum. But around his leader, he exhibited a slight inferiority complex quality, as though he always needed to prove something to Isagana. Still, he was a mean bastard.

"Around them?" he asked, tilting his head back at the scientists.

"Yes," Isagana said. His tone was sharp.

"Okay. Vergel's team never made it back from the disposal site," Rodrigo explained.

"I'm assuming you've tried radioing him?"

"Yes. No answer. It is possible it could be radio interference, but…"

"How long have they been gone?" Isagana said.

"Six hours," Rodrigo said. The group passed through the lobby. Two of the terrorists were seated in front of the large screen television. They had hooked up a video-game console and were playing *Grand Theft Auto*. They shouted obscenities to each other as they blasted NPCs with their digital avatars.

Isagana shrugged. "They may just be running late. It has been a while since we've been over there. And you can't travel more than thirty miles an hour going inland without blowing a tire." He sighed. "Damn it. That's probably what happened."

"Isagana, there's more," Rodrigo continued. "We haven't been able to reach the harbor. We've tried radioing but haven't heard anything."

"What about the runway site? They have better range."

"Nothing from them either," Rodrigo said. He pulled up his phone. "And we have this." Isagana took the iPhone from him and looked at the image. It was a plane. Despite being high in the air, he recognized that it was a military style jet. He zoomed in. He couldn't see a label on the aircraft to confirm who it was but he did recognize something else.

"When was this taken?"

"One of the men spotted it this morning while out on vehicle patrol."

"Any jumpers? Parachutes?"

"Not that he could see. That was when we tried raising the guards at the harbor," Rodrigo said. Isagana studied the picture again.

"They're at ten-thousand feet," he said. "That's the altitude I would want to make a parachute jump from." His glare intensified as he turned and looked at Bischoff. "You know anything about this, Doctor?"

"No. Nothing!" Bischoff said, trying his best to sound calm. He raised his voice to exude a sense of finality, "Of course not!"

"You sure? I know you think you are a clever man, Dr. Bischoff," Isagana said. "Perhaps you got word out somehow."

"I. Did. Not."

"We'll have to see," Isagana said.

They stepped outside. The area beyond the patio was relatively flat, having been cleared out during the construction process. It was a square-mile of open region, surrounded by a perimeter of jungle. At the east side dead ahead was the trail. A metal gate had been set up between the trees. The trail split past the gate, leading to two parking lots, simply referred to as the north and east lots. The north lot had the two Army cargo trucks, large vehicles capable of carrying over twenty troops at a time.

Parked beside them were a couple of Jeeps, which were used mainly for patrols. There were four Jeeps remaining in the east lot.

Behind the facility were three military-style tents set up for the men. Red Cobras patrolled the perimeter, with three or four of them further out within the trees.

Bischoff glanced to his left, seeing the cargo trucks parked in the north lot. Further around the building was the greenhouse. It was a facility that was almost twice as large as the maintenance building. Inside were hundreds of exotic plant species from around the globe. Every time he stepped outside, it was hard for the doctor to look at that greenhouse. There rested the remains of his true projects: his destiny that originally brought him to this island. He was nearly successful in his goals before the terrorist group tracked him down. The subjects, having been left unattended in the past six weeks, had wilted and died.

Bischoff fought against the urge to cough. The air smelled of pesticide poisoning. Paulo had been spraying relentlessly to keep the bug population down. His idea of a quick spray was to completely soak the surrounding jungle in poison. For a guy that had been exposed to rough conditions, he seemed ridiculously sensitive to mosquitoes.

"What should we do, Isagana?" Rodrigo asked.

"We investigate," Isagana asked. "I will take some men and check out the disposal site. Rodrigo, you stay here and keep an eye out. Have everyone on alert. I want a unit to go check out the harbor and see what's going on."

"Sir, we don't know how many are there," Rodrigo asked. "And I don't know how many men I can take off the site to investigate."

"That's why you'll take her as a hostage," Isagana said and pointed to Jean. Trevor and Bischoff gasped, the former aggressively stepping forward.

"You won't dare…"

Another blow from Paulo knocked him back to the ground. The Cobra immediately turned to face Jean. He held his hands up, taunting her to jump to Trevor's defense.

"You're pushing your luck, Doctor Malloy," Isagana warned. Trevor pushed himself off the ground, spitting dirt from his mouth.

"You want a hostage? Take me," he pleaded.

"No," Isagana said. "You will stay here. In the shack."

"Take me then," Dr. Bischoff said, hoping his status would help protect Jean from being in a possible crossfire.

"That's the plan, actually," Isagana said. "You're coming with *me* to the disposal site. Paulo, you lead a team to the harbor. Two Jeeps. Have someone on the radio at all times."

"You got it, boss," Paulo said. He stepped back into the building and yelled at the group of terrorists huddled by the television. "Hey! Gear up! We're moving out!" The crowd broke apart as the Cobras grabbed their rifles and filed out into the patio.

Trevor and Jean locked eyes for a moment before several men grabbed him by the arms and dragged him to the shack. He yelped as his leg was dragged across the dirt. Jean flinched as she felt Paulo's hand on her shoulder. He made sure that Trevor could see them.

"Don't worry, babe, we'll have a fun ride together." As he intended, Trevor yelled out in anger, only to have his calls muffled by the slamming of a wooden door. Paulo laughed. "Better hope there's nobody out there, because if there are, somebody will have ants in their pants PERMANANTLY."

He pushed Jean toward the east lot, then shoved Jean into the backseat of one of the Jeeps. He took the seat beside her, keeping his gun pressed into her ribs while two more men boarded into the front seats, and four others piled into the Jeep parked behind them. The driver floored the gas pedal, kicking up dirt as they sped out onto the trail.

"WHOO!" Paulo cheered.

As they sped off into the eastbound trail, Isagana and several other terrorists piled into a cargo truck. The men piled into the back along with the doctor while Isagana sat in the front passenger seat. He looked back at Rodrigo.

"You radio us at the first sign of trouble! Understand?"

"Yes sir," Rodrigo said. The driver started the engine and accelerated the truck into the inland trail, going northeast toward the center of the island. Bischoff rocked in the seat as the truck bumped over the dirt road. He cringed at the sound of Trevor's screams. The ants were already biting him. Knowing Rodrigo, he would not let him out until the Commander returned.

CHAPTER 7

"Ow! Son of a bitch," Yellowstone whispered. He slapped the mosquito that bit his neck, crushing it against his skin. He could hear the restrained chuckles from his teammates behind him.

"Having trouble up there?" Steele said.

"Apparently I taste good," Yellowstone complained. Banana-shaped leaves struck his face as he continued through the jungle. Flies as large as strawberries flew into him like kamikazes. He twisted as another mosquito bit the back of his neck. "Christ! Do these bugs know there's six other blood bags out here?"

"Maybe they smell all that food on you," Muddler said.

"It could just be mating season for them," Stroud joked.

"Explains why they're avoiding your ugly face," Rob chipped in. The team shared a moment of soft laughter. It was the first time anyone spoke since leaving the harbor.

The team continued on in silence. Yellowstone swatted bugs as he continued, while Muddler patrolled just a few feet to his right. She kept watch on the ground in search of signs for tripwires and other traps. They had traveled two miles in so far and there had been nothing, not even on the road. Judging by the way the Red Cobras had set up their foothold on the island, they assumed any attack would come from the coastline, hence the defenses guarding the trail.

The silence was still bothering her. They hadn't heard a single thing since they had entered the jungle. There was hardly a single birdsong. No monkeys or reptiles. There was only the annoying buzzing of insects, who seemed happy to give Yellowstone some company.

"That scientist...Dr. Bischoff? What was he experimenting on?" she asked, glancing back at Rob. He was in the middle of the group, his eyes never blinking as he watched through the thick jungle.

"Not exactly sure," he answered. "Some sort of biological experiment. I don't really know the details. All I know is he has skills or research that Isagana wants."

That info, as vague as it was, made her nervous. She had been in many jungles all over the world and none seemed as lifeless as this. Despite the golden rays of sunshine beaming through the canopy, there was a haunted quality about this place. Whatever was wrong, she didn't know what it was, and that bothered her more than all the hellholes she had spent months at a time in.

Yellowstone stopped and held his fist up, signaling the group to halt. They kneeled into firing stances, unsure of what the big guy had seen. After several moments of stillness, Yellowstone signaled to Rob.

"Spread out," he ordered the group. They branched out until there was twenty feet of space between them. Rob stepped up next to Yellowstone. "What is it? What do you see?"

Yellowstone nudged his head toward the ground. Rob looked. There was a long streak of blood in the grass. It was still wet, retaining its natural red color, which meant it wasn't very old. The grass had been pressed down, the dirt somewhat minced as though several rakes had been dragged through it. The trail originated somewhere to the left beyond their line of sight and continued on toward the Jeep trail. Rob looked at the trees and bushes, seeing scratches in the bark and roots. Several ferns and tall grass had been flattened, their leaves marked with the blood. Rob took a few steps and followed the blood to the tree line and stopped. It continued across the Jeep trail in thick streams. It seemed that something, or someone, had been dragged through here recently.

"Should we check it out?" Yellowstone asked.

"Yes," Rob answered.

"It could be anything," Valentine whispered. "It's a jungle. It's probably a cougar or a jaguar that got itself some dinner."

"There's no cats on these islands," Rob corrected him. "I want two men guarding here. Warn us if anyone comes. Everyone else, on me. Watch your backs. We're not alone in these woods."

Tire-man and Valentine held their position on this side of the trail while the others crossed the clearing. Muddler watched the blood, seeing ants and bugs feeding off the thicker globs. There were tiny flakes of flesh in the dirt, which appeared as though they had been scraped off the body they came from.

Rob was the first to enter the tree line on the other side of the trail. He waited at the tree line and cautiously looked into the jungle. So far, there was no movement. He shouldered his rifle, keeping his eye near the scope. The grass had been flattened, making the trail easy to follow. It was bent outward, meaning whatever passed through had gone in this direction.

After several yards, Rob noticed a small clearing in the distance. The ferns and grass had been scraped out by the roots, resulting in a black mound of dirt. Whatever it was, the trail led directly to it. Rob, Yellowstone, and Muddler took a triangular position, with the heavy gunner in front, while Steele and Stroud branched outward to flank any possible threat. The center group moved in and entered the clearing.

"What the shit?" Yellowstone muttered. He gazed down at the massive hole in the ground. The dirt had been dug out, forming a circle of residue around the pit as though he was looking at a four-foot-tall anthill. The dirt itself had colors of black and brown, meaning it contained soil from different depths.

Stroud and Steele emerged from behind the pit.

"Nobody out there as far as we can see," Steele said. He gazed at the big pit. "Anyone care to explain what this is?"

"It's a big hole," Yellowstone said.

"No shit, *Sherlock*. You win intellectual-of-the-year," Steele said. "No, I mean *this*?" He was pointing down at the edge of the pile. Rob walked around the strange mound, following the trail of blood that circled it. The trail expanded into a huge blood puddle surrounded by bits of bone and flesh.

"I have no idea," Rob said. The graveyard was vast, trailing far out into the jungle. It was like a waste deposit site for organic remains. There were some bits of flesh still stuck to the skeletons. The blood stained the entire side of the mound. Here, much of it was dry. "Whatever did this, it's been on a hunting spree. Not all of this blood was from whatever had been dragged."

"Yeah, how do you know that?"

"That blood we saw was fresh. But most of this isn't," Rob said.

"You don't mean to tell me the Red Cobras are living in tunnels and caves, do you?" Muddler said.

"No," Rob said with a brief chuckle. The smile quickly disappeared as his mind tried to fathom what he was looking at. There were skeletons from all different kinds of species discarded about. There were elephant seals, warthogs, monkeys, some large species of birds.

Then there was a pile of remains that completely caught him off guard. Rob stepped closer to examine them. They weren't flesh and definitely were not made of bone. It was fabric.

The clothes were almost unrecognizable both due to the bloodstains and the fact that they had been torn to ribbons. The fabric was a combination of tactical pants and some military-colored shirts. Laying among the pile was an empty gun belt and a pair of boots, each as torn up as the clothes.

Steele passed by him and knelt down near the clothing. He found a stick and started prodding the ribbons, mixing them as though stirring a soup. The stick connected with something hard. He peeled the clothes back, revealing the red-white bone of a human arm.

Steele jumped away, dropping the stick as though it had been tarnished by the touch.

"Now, that's DEFINITELY not normal."

"Uhh...if we keep looking at this boneyard, can we expect to find a human ribcage or pelvis?" Yellowstone replied.

"Who knows," Rob said. Muddler stared at the boneyard and back at the mound. Her stomach was feeling tight with anxiety. Now the silence of the jungle was REALLY bothering her.

"You said that doctor was working on biological experiments?"

"Get a grip," Rob said, sensing the nervousness in her voice. He avoided the question and kept looking.

"I've heard of fire ants that make huge anthills. They've been known to bring down animals as large as horses. They'll take 'em to these nests and strip them down to the bone," Yellowstone said. "Maybe that's what this is."

"In that case, I vote we hightail it," Muddler said.

"Wait, hang on," Steele said. "First, we find the cliffside and harbor settlements abandoned and in shambles. Now we find this, and you're not suspecting a connection?"

"I *do* suspect a connection," Rob said, his voice hard. "What do you expect me to do about it? It's a big hole. It's nothing to get worked...up...about..." his voice trailed off as he looked further out into the jungle. Beyond the trees was a large mass in the trees. Whatever it was, it was obscured by a wall of tall ferns and bamboo.

Rob walked past the clearing and entered the section of woods. This area was darker as the canopy above was thicker. The mercenaries followed and surrounded the object.

It was a Jeep, laying on its driver's side. Its windshield was heavily cracked and its front tires flattened. Blood crusted on the seats and dashboard. Steele took his machete and started cutting away some of the vines that clung to the wheels and doors.

"Has it been here a while?" Stroud asked.

"No," Steele said. "A lot of these vines have been pulled. It's almost like they drove blindly through the jungle and got snagged on all of this shit."

"Drove, huh?" Muddler said. "Then how do we account for that?" She pointed at the dirt bunched at the headlight and side, then at the trail of smothered plants behind the vehicle. Ferns and grass had been mashed

38

into the dirt. The trail was as wide as the vehicle itself, eliminating any doubt that it had been dragged by something.

"I don't suppose Isagana was in the habit of making big piles of dirt and dragging Jeeps through the jungle for no reason…was he?" Steele remarked. Rob examined the soil and the state of the uprooted grass.

"This was done recently," he said. He glanced back at the top of the vehicle. There were several deep groves in the hood, frame, doors, and top. He looked back at the deep dark trail where the Jeep had been dragged, then back at the strange mound of dirt. Now he was nervous. Though he wasn't sure what all of this meant, it was obvious that something had gone terribly wrong on this island. "Get back to the Jeep trail."

"We heading back?" Stroud asked.

"I'm making up my mind," Rob said. "But right now, I want everyone to stay together."

"Yes, boss," Yellowstone said. The group quickly hustled out of the dark section of jungle and moved in a tight bend around the strange mound, each of them giving it a final glance as they passed it by.

Its sensory receptors had detected several vibrations up on the surface. The arachnid quickly tucked the fresh victim into the deep channel of its lair before moving up to investigate. It had to have the victim properly placed for its dear Empress.

Razor claws at the end of its eight legs pulled it up through the tunnel. Dim rays of sunlight beamed down into its twelve eyes as it climbed the vertical path. It emerged from the mouth of its lair. Whatever had caused the vibrations had passed. The drone was too late. It removed itself from the hill, dragging its exhausted tail behind it. It had spent a lot of energy on this day, as it would for each day in the rest of its life. It lived to serve and to feed until the day its body would become too weak to function and thus conclude its final purpose, serving as sustenance for the younger members of its species.

Such a thing was for later. Now, preserving the species was its primary goal. It was a hunter. Until the day it would be consumed by its brethren, that was its function.

But its energy was low after its long journey from the water. Until its body recovered, it would have to remain stationary for now and lay in wait for any unsuspecting prey that came nearby. The arachnid scurried into the jungle for several yards and climbed a tree.

Concealed in the canopy, it waited patiently.

CHAPTER 8

The wind blasted in through the open window, assaulting Jean's hair. She brushed her hand over her forehead, peeling strands of hair from her face. She twisted in her seat, trying to back away from the muzzle of Paulo's submachine gun. The obnoxious terrorist continued to prod the weapon into her ribs, knowing full well it was bothering her.

She kept her eyes forward, not giving him the satisfaction of looking his way. She knew he was eyeing her figure, particularly her cleavage, and *wanted* to invoke a reaction out of her. The continuous prodding was a sign of his impatience.

With a smile, the terrorist prodded the weapon harder.

"God!" Jean finally shouted, instinctually raising a hand part way, as though to smack. The three terrorists in the Jeep laughed in unison. The front passenger turned back and laughed at her.

"What's the matter, baby?"

The look in their eyes disturbed her. It didn't take much intelligence to know that these men hadn't been around a woman in a long time…and not just because of their line of work. She looked away from him and tried to focus on the array of jungle outside her window. They were a little more than halfway to the beach, yet, these sickos seemed to be focused on something else.

She flinched as Paulo ran the gun muzzle along her inner thigh.

"I don't think Isagana would care for what you're thinking," she warned. Paulo raised the weapon to her chest and kept it pointed, as though cautioning her, then proceeded to push the muzzle into the corner of her blouse. It was obvious that this group was not too concerned with the lack of communication from the harbor. More than likely, they suspected it was just communication failure. She held her breath, trying hard not to display any reaction.

"Isagana wants you to complete his experiment," Paulo said. "He doesn't care about what else occurs in the meantime."

"She's not producing results," the driver said. "Might as well make her good for something."

"We should have brought your boyfriend along to watch," Paulo said. He started to laugh. "Perhaps we can film it with an iPhone and show him the video."

"It's your choice," she warned. She spoke casually as though addressing unruly high schoolers. Her remark prompted further laughter. Paulo slowly pushed her shirt further, revealing the golden skin on her chest. He leaned up, allowing himself full view of her cleavage. He smiled, exposing those cracked, rotting teeth. She was a C-cup at best, but he had seen worse. Her athletic figure more than made up for it.

"I appreciate the warning," he said. He reached to touch with his other hand.

"Appreciate *this*." She shifted her weight to the right and threw her hand out, landing a chop to his throat. Paulo gagged and flailed frantically as the doctor pulled the gun from his grip. Despite his airway closing off, he lunged at her to get it back.

Jean shoved an elbow to his jaw, breaking his already cracked teeth. Paulo reel backward until he hit the door. With one final yank, the gun came free of his hand.

She pressed the gun into the back of the driver's seat and fired. The terrorist driver convulsed as though struck by lightning. Exit wounds tore open his chest, spraying his blood onto the dashboard. His body leaned forward against the wheel, his weight pressing his foot on the pedal. The Jeep swerved then slowly started to coast to the left.

Paulo's eyes opened wide as the he saw the gun's smoking muzzle turn toward him. He pulled the handle open and fell out of the moving Jeep. He bounced and rolled as he connected with the dirt road. The trailing Jeep swerved to the right to avoid hitting him then stopped. The passengers opened the doors, ready to check on him.

"Go!" he said, spitting blood with each word. The way he frantically pointed at the other Jeep, they knew something had gone wrong. The group ducked back into the Jeep and sped off in pursuit.

The front passenger reached for the wheel, trying to keep the Jeep from going off the road. In the corner of his eye, he saw Jean pointing the weapon at him. Unable to aim his rifle in the tight quarters, he reached for his pistol. His fingers barely touched the grip as Jean put a barrage of bullets through his chest and neck.

He slumped back against the dashboard, his eyes exhibiting shock before the life passed from his body.

41

For a moment, Jean found herself staring at what she had just done. It had been a decade since she had pointed a weapon at anyone. Yet, somehow, it felt like yesterday.

That moment of reflection was over as soon as it started. The Jeep shook as it started rolling off the trail. Jean looked up through the battered windshield just in time to see the tree twenty feet ahead. She turned and braced for impact.

The Jeep smashed into the tree, imploding the engine. Jean hit the back of the driver's seat with her shoulder. Shards of glass whipped by her head like grenade shrapnel. She straightened her posture and unbuckled the belt. She got out of the Jeep and stepped into a wall of ferns that stood as high as her head. She moved to the driver's seat with the intention of collecting the dead terrorists' weapons but stopped as the second vehicle approached.

"Shit," she muttered. She raised Paulo's submachine gun and fired into the windshield. The driver cut the wheel hard, inadvertently sending the vehicle off the trail and into another tree. All four doors opened at once. Jean fired another burst, peppering the passenger side. Another squeeze of the trigger resulted in a dull *click*. The magazine was spent. The only other option now was to run.

She dropped the weapon and darted into the jungle as fast as she could. The terrorists bolted from the vehicle, with Paulo trailing several yards behind.

"Get that bitch!" he yelled.

****

"What do we do, Boss?" Valentine asked. The team assembled where the blood trail crossed the Jeep trail. Rob shook his head. He had explained to Val and Tire-man what they had found, and they too were feeling apprehensive about pushing forward without sufficient data.

"I might have to make a call and…" he stopped, looking back into the jungle. The team heard it too. Rattling sounds…popping sounds…rapid gunfire!

"We might have our intel right there!" Valentine said.

"Let's move!" Rob ordered. The team ran into the jungle and converged onto the noise. The shooting had stopped, now replaced by the shouting of orders. Rob recognized the accents. No doubt these guys were Red Cobras.

****

"Get her! Get her!" one of the four Cobras yelled as they chased Jean through a tight grouping of trees.

The chemist pushed off her heel, weaving between the enormous obstacles in her path. Thick bushes and low hanging branches slapped against her clothes. She hopped over a series of exposed roots and bamboo, landing on the bottom of a small hill. She glanced back, catching glimpses of her pursuers moving between the trees.

She started up the hill, slipping on mud with her foot step. She stopped her fall with her hands and righted herself. Several shots rang out. Dirt kicked up simultaneously all around her, spurring her to move faster. These maniacs were out for blood now.

Jean came to the top of the hill, nearly colliding with the base of a tree. Bullet holes exploded along the trunk, twelve inches away from her head.

"God!" Jean leapt back, her heel catching on a series of vines. She rolled backward head over heels down the small slope of the hill until hitting the base of another tree. Sneering in pain, she pushed herself up. By now, the Cobras were passing over the top of the hill.

"There!" one of them yelled. All four Cobras quickly descended and surrounded her.

"Where are you?!" Paulo yelled out somewhere in the jungle.

"Down here! We got her!" one of the Cobras called back. A set of hands grabbed Jean under the arms and lifted her to her feet. His three comrades closed in, each of them bearing the same angry facial expression. Their eyes were burning with both lust and rage.

"You will regret doing that," the terrorist holding her whispered in her ear. One of his comrades laid his rifle on the ground and moved his hands to his belt buckle.

"Me first!" he declared.

"Paulo will be pissed," the one holding her replied.

"Paulo should've moved faster." The terrorist unfastened the buckle. Jean twisted, then stopped as she felt the tip of a knife prod into her waist as a warning to quit struggling. She sucked in a breath as the terrorist proceeded to unbutton his pants.

A shot rang out and the flesh near his groin exploded. The terrorist's mouth gaped wide in shock. A three-round burst echoed, and in that same moment, three bullets tore his chest open, driving him to the ground.

The two terrorists behind him pointed their guns into the jungle in search of where the shots came from. Jean felt the Cobra holding her twist and look behind him, slightly loosening his hold. She seized the opportunity and tucked down, slipping under his grasp. The terrorist turned back and reached for her.

His eye caught the glimpse of a silver object spiraling out of the trees. His lungs deflated as the six-inch blade plunged into his chest. The terrorist sank to his knees, clutching the handle that protruded from his chest.

Rob stepped out of the trees with his H&K in hand. He would not have to waste any bullets on this scum, as his throw had hit its mark precisely. The hostile slumped to the side, dead. Just a yard beside him was the hostage. Several feet behind her were two more hostiles.

Their attention was on him…just as he planned. The one at his ten-o'clock never noticed Muddler emerging behind him with her knife raised high. She brought it down, plunging the blade through his neck.

The last remaining member of the group saw his comrade go down. Realizing he was outmatched, he turned to run, only to come face-to-face with Steele. He had both his machete and combat knife drawn.

"Hello there!" the mercenary said, grinning ear to ear. He rammed the machete into the Cobra's belly, running it deep until the blade jutted out his back. The terrorist gagged, his eyes wide with pain. With the enemy still impaled on the machete, Steele raised his smaller knife and stabbed deep into his neck, finishing him off.

Paulo followed the trail up the hill. He heard the interchange of his men, meaning they had caught the hostage. Then there was a burst of gunfire, followed by the faint sounds of some sort of conflict.

By the time he neared the top of the hill, his team had been completely slaughtered. Their killers were heavily armed and clearly well-trained. Paulo turned away and retreated.

Isagana was right. That plane in the photo had deployed a task force to eliminate their stronghold. Knowing they would easily intercept him on the Jeep trail, he decided to flee deeper into the jungle.

Jean looked around, shocked to see the seven mercenaries appearing out of the jungle. They formed a perimeter while Rob helped her to her feet.

"Relax, we're here to help," he said. "Are there any others nearby?"

"One more," she said. She pointed back over the hill. "Paulo. Back there somewhere!"

CHAPTER 9

In just a few moments, Paulo felt he had run so fast he may as well have crossed the island. In actuality, he only made a few hundred meters. In those moments, he stumbled almost a dozen times. The terrain threw every obstacle it had at him. There was no line of sight. The jungle only got thicker the further in he went.

He stopped and looked back, gripping his sidearm with both hands. From what he could tell, the task force wasn't following him. He briefly debated the thought of making his way back to the Jeeps. The second one didn't appear to be too badly damaged.

No. Too late for that.

By now the mercenaries had probably secured that location anyway. His best course of action would be to make his way to the harbor. It was his only way of alerting base camp, unless the mercenaries trashed the radio tower. Paulo stopped pondering the possibilities and resumed his retreat. Honor was out the window. He had no intention of going down guns-blazing in a fight he couldn't win. Isagana would call him a coward, but he didn't care. Cowards often lived longer than the brave.

He tore through a series of bushes, sending leaves and twigs twirling through the air like confetti. He only made another step to the other side as the shoulder strap on his vest snagged on something, yanking him into a crazed spiral. The branch or whatever it was snapped and he fell clumsily down a small slope.

Paulo lifted his dirt covered face out of the ground and looked at his empty hands. His pistol had been accidentally flung into the distance. He had heard it land, giving him a general sense of direction. He absolutely DID NOT want to go through this jungle unarmed.

The arachnid could sense movement below. Claws located on the end of its eight legs kept a firm grip on the tree, while its enormous pincers opened. Very slowly, it cocked both arms back, putting the pincers near its head. Its tail coiled, its stinger quivering as it generated venom. It was hidden perfectly in the canopy, ready to ambush the unsuspecting prey.

Paulo kept one hand on his knife. He knew it wouldn't do him much good against the mysterious attackers, but it made him feel better nonetheless. He kept a low posture as he walked, hoping to remain undetected from the strike team. He glanced back again, seeing nothing but green behind him.

Up ahead he saw a small clearing. The ground had been minced as though something huge had been dragged through the jungle. Paulo slowly followed the strange trail for several yards until he saw the Jeep laying on its side.

"Patrol Team six?" He briefly examined the Jeep and its intense damage, noticing a bit of red spray paint near the rear. It was definitely Team Six's patrol vehicle. He had gambled with these men. Hell, one of them owed him a large sum of money.

He heard movement somewhere behind him. He drew his knife and turned with it raised in a combat position. He waited for someone to emerge out of the jungle.

Nothing.

He glanced down at his knife, then shook his head, realizing how foolish he looked. Like that knife would do him any good against multiple men with automatic weapons. After a few moments of silence, he decided once again to retreat. He found himself in the clearing, and in the middle of a boneyard. He gasped, seeing the bones of several different species. Worms crawled through the eye sockets and ribcages of warthogs, seals, monkeys, and birds. His eyes went to the huge anthill-like mound, seeing the blood that trailed the side.

He gradually backed out of the clearing. In doing so, his foot bumped another skeleton. He gazed down, immediately seeing the empty eyes of a human skull. Its body lay disjointed, the mouth agape as though still screaming in terror.

Paulo yelped and hurried out of the clearing into the trees.

A strange hissing overtook the silence. He froze, seeing nothing moving between the plants. The hissing was then joined by the sound of scraping wood. It was then that he realized that whatever it was, it was not on the ground, but up in the trees.

Paulo saw the frolicking mandibles and the twelve marble eyes above them. He yelled and tried to run but was too late.

The creature sprung from its post and landed directly on him. Paulo squealed as bony claws clamped down on his arms, pinning him down. Its shell was rigid, yet had a wet, slimy texture to it. It tucked its head back, pointing its twelve eyes at his face. The tail arched over its head and lowered the stinger toward his flesh. Paulo struggled one final time as the tip entered his neck.

A muffled yell left his lungs. His voice slurred as the venom did its work. He tried to push the creature away but his arms wouldn't move. The creature scurried off of him and moved to his feet. He was on the ground looking up. His mind worked but his body didn't.

There was pain at his ankles as the claws clamped down. His body trembled as it was dragged through the grass, through the boneyard, and up that horrible mound. The arachnid adjusted its grip and carried him deep into the tunnel.

Then there was darkness.

CHAPTER 10

"Nothing," Muddler said, shaking her head. She and Yellowstone trekked for nearly a half a mile but found nothing. The trail ran cold near the mound. Yellowstone was several feet in the tree line looking at the ground. There were several abrasions in the dirt as though a struggle had taken place recently. His eyes glanced up to the bizarre mound.

She noticed some blood. Immediately, she began to question in her mind if that was there before. She gazed back to the ground. In the grass, staring back at her, was a human skull.

That uneasy feeling in her gut returned.

"Let's go back," she said.

****

Jean sat in the backseat of the vacant Jeep as Valentine applied some disinfectant to the scratches on her arms.

"Can't let that go untreated out here," he said. "Infection even from this would kill ya."

"Thanks. I've only been on this island *three months*," Jean quipped. Valentine smiled and closed the med-kit. She stood up and noticed Rob inspecting the bodies of the other Jeep.

"Did you learn to do *this* in those three months?" he asked, sounding impressed. Jean tore at the rip in her sleeve, ripping the whole thing off revealing her upper arm. Tattooed on her arm was a pair of U.S. Air Force wings.

"Had to pay for my degree somehow," she said.

"Let me guess: Iraq? Pararescue Division?" Steele said.

"That's right," she said.

"I see," Rob said. He held out his hand, formally introducing himself. "Rob Cashen."

"Dr. Jean Kyunghee." They shook hands. "You guys obviously are private contractors."

"That we are. The Philippine government contacted us and issued a contract on Isagana. They can't move in here with a military force to take a stab at Isagana, with this island so close to Hawaii. They won't ask the U.S. for assistance because...well...they want to keep this as quiet as possible."

"Quiet? What's so special about Isagana?"

"In a nutshell, he's just a common terrorist," Rob said. "Problem is he's already bombed a Japanese science facility and had plans to hit an embassy in Beijing. Apparently, he was a General in the Philippine military and an advisor to their president. He wanted to expand their military and take over the Japanese Islands. My understanding is that his grandfather was tortured in World War Two and he holds a grudge."

"I see. So, the government doesn't want to ask the U.S. to send the Navy SEALs in. If so, word might get out that the Philippine President's advisor nearly created the next *ISIS*."

"Something like that," Rob said.

"More money for us," Stroud said.

"How many of your people are left?" Rob asked Jean.

"Two. Dr. Trevor Malloy and Dr. Bischoff," she answered. "Our facility is almost four miles inland. We're gonna want to strike soon. Isagana departed with a squad to investigate some missing Cobras near a ridge in the center of the island. This squad here were going to check up on the guys you bagged at the harbor." Rob and Steele shared a glance. Stroud, Tire-man, and Valentine stood silent, uncertain of what to say. She noticed the confusion on their faces. "Is...there a problem?"

"We don't know," Rob said. "The construction and harbor fortifications were already neutralized upon our arrival."

"That's a mild way to put it," Valentine said. "Torn to shit is how I'd say it."

"What?!" Jean exclaimed. "What happened? Is there another strike team?"

"Not that we know of. The situation isn't like anything we've seen," Rob said. "Listen Doctor, we know Dr. Bischoff has been working on biological experiments and that Isagana wanted to weaponize his research. Clearly this island was chosen because it was isolated. I have to ask, was there some sort of outbreak here? Anything that you're aware of?"

"What? No! Not at all. That's not the kind of experiments we were doing," she said.

Their conversation was interrupted by the arrival of Muddler and Yellowstone. Muddler was shaking her head as she approached Rob.

"Can't find him."

"What do you mean you can't find him?" Rob said.

"The trail went cold," Muddler said.

"Right by the boneyard," Yellowstone added.

"Boneyard?" Jean exclaimed. It was apparent she wasn't aware of it or the mysterious mound.

"I don't know what the case is, Doc, but there's something weird going on," Rob said. "The fortunate thing is that we know now that there are survivors. That means we can press on."

"Good. Let's get this over with," Valentine said. "This place is giving me the creeps."

"Thought somebody with a black heart wasn't afraid of anything," Muddler said.

"That somebody just doesn't like surprises," Valentine said.

"Hey Val, I have a *surprise* gift for you," Rob said. "You get to drive this Jeep. Tire-man, check that engine and see if it'll still run."

"Drive? We going for a ride?" Valentine asked.

"For starters. Then, we'll give the Red Cobras back their rides," Rob said. Tire-man popped the hood and inspected the engine. Rob snapped his fingers at Yellowstone, prompting him to step forward. "Unpack your explosives and load some up in these Jeeps. We'll give these bastards their vehicles back with a little something extra."

"You got it, Boss," Yellowstone said.

"Whatever you do, it better be fast. If that guy's out there, he's gonna try and find a way to alert the rest of the terrorists," Jean said.

"Trust me, he's got a plan," Yellowstone said. He opened up an interior pouch in the bag that carried his M60 and pulled out a few blocks of C4. As he loaded them into the Jeep, Jean opened the front passenger seat and pulled the assault rifle from the dead Cobra's lap. Rob watched as she checked the magazine and pulled the cocking mechanism. "What do you think you're doing, Doc?"

"I'm not gonna sit by and watch. I'm gonna help," she said.

"Oh, no you're not!" Rob said. "We're getting paid on the condition we put Isagana down...and bring you back ALIVE. Putting you in the line of fire isn't complementary to that objective."

"I understand that, Mr. Cashen. But I'm absolving you of that decision," she said. "Those bastards have my fiancé locked in a shed full of ants. I know the layout of the facility. I've studied the patrols and routines the Cobras have been following."

"I believe you. The answer's still no." He yanked the rifle out of her hand.

"Hey!" she exclaimed. She made a move to grab it, only for Rob to twist her wrist, lock her arm, and drive her back in a single smooth motion.

"And respectfully, you don't have the authority to absolve me of anything. *I* make the tactical decisions here. And I'm not bringing you along." He let go. Jean massaged her wrist, grimacing back at him.

"I don't know, boss. She might be of help. She did good with these bastards here," Tire-man said, pointing down at the dead terrorists.

"Try all you want. She's not interested in you," Rob retorted. Tire-man scowled and resumed twisting a screwdriver into the engine.

"Where's she gonna go?" Muddler asked. "I'm not too comfortable with having her wait by the harbor."

"Considering what happened to that Jeep over there, I'm not sure she should be left anywhere unguarded. And splitting us up wouldn't do any good," Tire-man said.

Rob shook his head, feeling outnumbered by his own team. "Is that engine fixed yet?" he said, trying to change the subject.

"It'll be clunky. But it should work long enough to get us where we need to go."

"There are scouts you'll have to get past," Jean warned. "They have people patrolling for almost a half mile out. I know where the guard posts are hidden."

Rob tensed and bit his lip. He hated the idea of bringing her along. But the fact of the matter was time was short and they needed to act fast. At least she had combat training and was no stranger to pointing a gun at somebody. On top of that she did have helpful intel.

"Fine," he said, handing the gun back to her. "You'll come with us but you're staying behind cover. My plans work because my team follows my instructions, and I don't need you screwing that up going all *Rambo* on these assholes. Deal?"

Jean accepted the AK-47.

"Deal."

Rob motioned for everyone to gather around him.

"Alright, here's the plan…"

CHAPTER 11

Tires kicked up dirt as the cargo truck pulled off to the side of the trail. All eyes went to the overturned Dodge pickup truck.

"That was Vergil's truck," the driver said as he brought the truck to a stop. Isagana stepped out and approached the Dodge. The windshield was smashed, the engine marked with several deep grooves. The passenger door looked as though it had been struck by a charging rhino.

The eight Cobras disembarked and formed a perimeter. Bischoff grunted in discomfort as one of them dragged him out by the collar. He gasped as he saw the ravaged vehicle and the blood on the windshield shards. The hairs on the back of his neck stood on end as he noticed Isagana's fierce gaze directed at him. It was as though Isagana personally blamed Bischoff for the loss of his men.

"What do you know of this?" the terrorist leader said.

Bischoff held his hands up in surrender. "I...I know nothing!" Isagana was stepping closer now.

"Did you make contact with the outside?"

"No! I swear!" Bischoff pleaded.

"Then how do you explain that aircraft? How do you explain *this*?" Isagana growled. He struck the doctor in the belly with the butt of his rifle. Bischoff groaned and fell to his knees. "Let me ask you again..."

Bischoff held a hand up as a plea for him to stop.

"Every first of the month, I contact the University funding my research regarding supplies and progress. Lately, I haven't made contact for obvious reasons. Undoubtedly, they tried to contact me, but we never received the signals because your men took over my radio tower." Dr. Bischoff looked the Cobra in the eye and stood up. He then looked at the Dodge teetering on its left side. His eyes focused on the bizarre indentation in the passenger side. "Plus, I'm not sure what could've done this."

One of the terrorists inspecting the wreckage looked to his commander.

"I see no bullet holes. No powder burns. Nothing," he said.

"Any bodies?"

"No. None."

"Why would someone hide the bodies but leave the truck here?" Bischoff said. Isagana considered striking him again, thinking the doctor was attempting to jerk him around. However, his point made sense, though he wouldn't admit it out loud.

The commander examined the ground. Footprints were scattered all over the dirt road leading to the tree line.

"They ran out here," he said.

"Should we investigate?" one of the men asked.

"They could be anywhere by now," Isagana said. "If they're even alive."

"What do we do?" another Cobra asked. Isagana thought for a moment, gazing at the truck and the strange markings in the trail behind it.

"We will return to the lab," he said. "Now that we have confirmed a threat level, we will set up defenses. Whoever's here, they won't dare to risk the hostages."

Bischoff swallowed hard as he listened to them. He studied the scene one more time. It didn't look anything like what a group of soldiers would do. There was no shrapnel or bullet holes in the truck. Unless they shot through the windshield and took out the driver. If the truck went off the road and sideswiped a tree, it would explain the damage, even though it still looked like it was hit dead on by something. Then again, he was no soldier and knew nothing about the tactics of rescue teams. Considering there was nothing on this island larger than a deer, the process of elimination led him to believe this had to be the result of a sneak attack.

And likely, the rescue party, whoever they were, were probably counting on the Reb Cobras being unaware of their presence. There had been no radio traffic, meaning no alerts had come in from Paulo's scout team. Small unsuspecting groups of terrorists were probably not particularly difficult to eliminate, even with a hostage involved. And knowing Paulo, he was more focused on Dr. Kyunghee's legs than responding to a possible threat. Bischoff thought of her and Dr. Malloy. He desperately wanted them rescued off this island. If Isagana made it back and alerted his forces, it would stifle the chances of a successful rescue.

Unless he did something.

Bischoff carefully looked back at the cargo truck. The engine was still running and no Cobras were standing beside it. Most of the men stood guard along the tree line near the Dodge, while Isagana and a couple others were still observing the trail of footprints. Only one stood guarding him, and even he seemed distracted by the crash site.

Bischoff slowly backed toward the truck, watching his guard carefully. His elbow bumped against the edge of the open door. Bischoff edged closer to it. Finally, the guard glanced to his right, realizing the hostage was not there. With a burst of energy, he turned and saw Bischoff. The doctor jumped into the driver's seat and slammed the door shut.

"HEY!" the guard yelled. The Cobras yelled and pointed their weapons. Bischoff ducked his head down and floored the accelerator. The truck took off like a rocket. Isagana dove into the jungle, narrowly avoiding being plowed by the LDT 465 six-cylinder engine.

Several assault rifles opened fire, pelting the side of the truck. Bischoff ducked his head low as he passed by the group, keeping the pedal floored the entire way. Glass shattered as bullets burst through the windows. He weaved left and right, struggling to stay on the trail.

Isagana sprang to his feet and aimed his assault rifle. The path was curving up ahead to the left. He aimed low as the truck reached the bend and fired a spray of bullets.

Bischoff had just turned the wheel to follow the curve as rubber exploded off the front wheel. The truck bounced hard against the uneven ground and swerved out of control. He twisted the wheel, veering back to the right, then again to the left. For a moment, it was as though he was driving on ice. He fought against the machine for another hundred yards until the road curved again. A wall of green waited ahead of him.

"Oh, shit!" he yelled. He slammed on the brakes but it was too late. The truck plowed into the jungle, tearing through brush and scraping against several trees before smashing into a log. Bischoff fell forward, bloodying his nose against the steering wheel. He opened the door and fell out of the truck. He was in a daze, though still bursting from adrenaline.

He grabbed onto the truck and pulled himself to his feet. Through the trail of ravaged jungle, he could see the Jeep trail. Isagana and his squad raced along the bend. He pointed at the newly created hole in the tree line and led a charge.

"There!" the terrorist yelled.

Dr. Bischoff took off running into the jungle interior. It was the fastest he had ever run since his youth. He wasn't the athletic type and it was showing. Already his lungs felt they were about to burst. Sweat pooled under his bandanna and streaked down his face. His shins and quads were burning and his feet ached.

Gunshots cracked through the jungle. He could hear the whistling sounds of bullets streaking through the jungle around him. Refusing to look back, he pushed through the pain and fatigue. He weaved around a thick tree then stumbled as it led to a steep hill. He twisted his body to the right and dug his heels into the dirt, barely keeping his balance as he descended down the incline.

Bischoff reached the bottom of the hill. Finally, he glanced back to gauge the distance between himself and the Red Cobras. So far, they had not reached the top of the hill, but he could hear their running footsteps closing in.

His foot hit something solid in the grass, causing him to tumble. His stomach hit something rigid as he came down. Whatever it was, it cracked under his trunk, causing him to roll forward. Surrounded by tall grass and bushes, he reached out to push himself up, grazing the hard object with his fingers. He'd been a scientist long enough to recognize the feel of decaying bone. He looked down, seeing the ribcage of a human skeleton laying on its back.

Gasping in panic, he leaped backward, only for his heel to crunch another set of bones. He turned and looked down, seeing another human skeleton embedded in the dirt. Military boots were still clutched to its feet, its hands still wearing gloves. Most of the clothing had been ripped off and scattered throughout the section of trees, where several other bones lay discarded.

In the middle of the grouping was a cone-shaped structure. It was made of soil. Standing six-feet high, it resembled a miniature volcano. In its center was a gaping hole large enough for a four-wheeler to fall through. Whatever it was, it had been formed possibly a month ago, judging by the decay all around it and the condition of the exposed soil.

"What in the name of…"

"THERE!" a voice yelled from behind him. Bischoff looked up, seeing the Red Cobras descending down the hill. He resumed his retreat on wobbly legs, spitting and heaving as he passed the mound and pressed further into the jungle.

Isagana hurdled over the series of bones as he pursued the hostage. He could see the doctor up ahead. His patience had worn dry. Isagana aimed his AKM and fired.

Bischoff heard the crack as he felt the bullet punch through his left leg just above the knee. His momentum drove him into a rolling tumble. He ended up on his back, looking up into the canopy above.

The Cobras spread out forming a perimeter. Isagana stood above the doctor.

"That was a foolish mistake you've made," he said. Bischoff said nothing. Squirming in agony, he leaned up and clutched his leg. His femur had been shattered, some of the bone exposed through the gaping wound. Isagana kicked him in the chin, knocking him on his back. With a sadistic grin, he raised his foot and slowly pressed it down on the wound. Bischoff screamed and twisted.

Isagana continued the torture for several seconds then stepped off of him. Bischoff gasped for breath and laid still. Silently, he prayed for death and gazed back up into the canopy. He always loved the tropics and the untouched green that defined these Pacific islands.

The sense of peace was replaced by confusion. Bischoff squinted. There was something moving within the branches. It was black, far larger than any primate known to live in this region.

Isagana leaned down, partly obstructing his view.

"I am NOT going to kill you," he said. It was not comfort but a threat of punishment. "We will kill these intruders and find a new place to work. Once we do, you will continue your work until you are successful. You will regret your actions of defiance, as you will not be the one to pay for them. That debt will go to Dr. Kyunghee, and believe me, it will not be quick and joyous for her."

Bischoff tilted his head, ignoring every word as he looked past the terrorist commander. His eyes widened in horror as the thing moved. Spider-like legs carried its body across the huge limb. A long, segmented tail coiled behind its elongated body. It turned and faced down. Two enormous pincer claws, like those of a crab, reared back by its ugly head.

Bischoff stuttered like a bumbling fool. He questioned if he was hallucinating. The confusion elevated to panic, causing him to hyperventilate. Isagana smirked, thinking the doctor was reacting to his threat.

"HELP!" one of his men screamed.

Something passed through the forest like a fleeting ghost. Scissor-like claws snatched the screaming terrorist and pulled him back behind a wall of bushes and ferns.

"What the—" Isagana said as the man disappeared. He pointed to three men gathered on his right. "You three, go after him! Everyone else, form a defense. It's that rescue party—"

Another scream caused him to turn around. Isagana staggered back as he saw the huge insectoid shape leaping, tackling another of his men to the ground. The Cobra clawed at the dirt, desperate to get away. The beast reached with its pincers and clamped down on his forearms. Shrieks of agony pierced the air as the claws effortlessly cut through flesh and bone, severing both his hands at once. In a lightning fast motion, the tail snapped down over the creature's face, repeatedly sticking him in the back.

Isagana opened fire. The creature jolted as several rounds punched through the exoskeleton on its back. With rapid motion, it grasped a firm hold of its victim and scurried back, disappearing into the jungle. Isagana chased it, spraying bullets until his magazine ran empty. He stared out into the jungle, unable to see the beast.

"What was that?!" one of the men yelled. Isagana reloaded and backtracked to the group.

"Pick him up!" he said, pointing at the doctor. "Let's get the hell out of here!"

Two Cobras gathered near the doctor and bent down to lift him up. Bischoff yelled.

"Shut up!" one of them snapped, believing he was fussing from the pain. They lifted him to his feet and realized he was pointing up at the canopy.

That black shape in the tree sprang down from its hiding position, knocking all three of them to the ground like dominoes. Bischoff yelled as his injured leg buckled under his weight. The terrorist to his left sprang to his feet and ran, only to be jumped by another of the black arachnid creatures. It wrestled with him, tangling its legs and arms over his body. They rolled repeatedly until finally its stinger arched down, repeatedly punching holes in his chest.

Bischoff felt flailing legs sweep over his body as the Cobra on his right wrestled with the creature that had sprung from the tree. Bischoff rolled away, hearing the Cobra's screams as the creatures plunged its pincers into his ribs like steak knives. The tail came down in a snapping motion. The screams turned into a bloody garble as the stinger sank into his throat.

Gunshots and screams filled the jungle. The terrorists had scattered, panicked and disorganized. The only one keeping his wits together was Isagana, who emptied a second magazine into the horde. The former General looked to the mound, seeing the bugs scurrying out of the huge mound one after another. In moments, there were over a dozen creatures converging on the group. They were everywhere, crawling up and down the trees like termites.

"Come on! Back to the truck!" he yelled, dashing into the woods. Four men followed, firing aimlessly into the trees. Bischoff reached out, pleading not to be left behind. The group of five ran into the distance in a single file.

Another black shape fell from the tree and landed on the unlucky Cobra in the back. Three hundred pounds drove him facedown into the dirt. Razor sharp pincers sliced into his flesh while the pointy stinger punched down. Isagana and the others disappeared into the jungle, abandoning their helpless comrades.

"No!" Bischoff groaned. It couldn't be real. He *had* to have been dreaming! His stomach tightened as the arachnids dragged the stiffened terrorists back to the huge mound.

He could hear several feet rustling the ground, drawing closer and closer behind him. Panic struck, spurring him to attempt crawling away. He pulled himself forward, only to feel the sharp pressure of claws compressing his legs. His arms stretched flat against the ground as the arachnid pulled him backward. He twisted and kicked with his good leg, rolling to his back. The creature reared on its back legs, agitated by the kicks. Mandibles unfolded, revealing choppers as sharp as the pincers.

Bischoff kicked again, his boot scraping against the rock-hard shell on its underbelly. Those pincers snapped down on his ankle. He yelled as the creature applied pressure. The ridged edge sliced through the tissue all the way to the bone. The pressure continued. Bischoff jolted back as the bone snapped like a twig. The creature moved up, its tail twitching behind its body.

"No! NO!" he pleaded, as though communicating with a compassionate lifeform.

The tail cracked down like a whip, piercing his belly. Venom flooded his body like an invading army. He felt his muscles tightening. It was almost as if electricity was surging through his body. His arms grew heavy, slumping at his sides after a few moments. In the end, only a few bodily functions remained. His heart beat slowly, his lungs inflating slowly, keeping him alive.

He panicked in silence, unable to speak. His scientific mind started to comprehend the horrors that were taking place. Whatever this venom did, it was designed to allow the brain to keep the heart beating and the lungs pumping oxygen, as though he were asleep. It was meant to keep him alive, which terrified him more than anything.

The terror intensified as the creatures dragged him up the mound, into the pit.

CHAPTER 12

With his AKM assault rifle gripped firmly in his hands, the Red Cobra patrolled the jungle. He was about a thousand feet from the complex and was about to complete his second pass over his designated area. He had been warned of possible intruders on the island and had seen Paulo's unit blast up the Jeep trail.

He watched the jungle intently, seeing the same bushes and trees he had passed by a thousand times in previous patrols. His throat was dry, causing him to cough every few moments. It was that damn pesticide that Paulo had been spraying. Thirty minutes until his patrol concluded. Thirty minutes having to breathe in this crap in the air! The idiot had completely overdone it and now he had to walk through the crap. God knows what it was doing to his lungs. But Isagana let it happen, thus, he would not complain.

As he kept on the path, he could see the rotting trunk of a fallen tree. Its collapse had created a void in the forest, giving him a direct view of the complex. It was here where he usually came across another patroller. They chatted about anything, ranging from venting about their commanders, talking about Dr. Kyunghee's anatomy, or sharing war stories of people they'd killed in various raids.

Like clockwork, his comrade was approaching from the opposite side. He was about thirty feet up ahead of him. They shared a wave and closed in on the log. The patroller lowered his rifle and prepared to make some small talk.

He stopped, seeing his comrade drop his rifle and clutch his throat. Something protruded from his neck. A black object…a knife handle!

The target stopped right where he wanted. Rob waited low behind a thick bush, waiting for the patroller to walk by. He was behind him now. Muddler's knife had taken out the other, drawing his attention. Rob had to strike now during the split moment where the target's brain was comprehending what was happening.

He lunged forward and cupped a hand over the Cobra's mouth. There was a brief struggle as he drove the knife deep into his jugular. The Cobra squirmed for a count of five then slowly slumped back against him.

Muddler emerged from her hiding place and pulled her knife free from the dead Cobra she slayed.

"That's the last of the patrols," Rob said. Muddler looked through the gap in the trees. The jungle was thick enough to provide cover for her, while still giving her a good line of sight. She could point out Cobras as they moved across the front lawn of the facility.

"Perfect spot for me," she said. She pulled her sniper rifle from her shoulder. She moved in front of the downed tree and set up the tripod support, then tested the scope. "I see the maintenance shed. I believe that's where Jean said they're holding her boyfriend."

"It is," Dr. Kyunghee said. She emerged from the jungle behind them. Rob grimaced, still not enthusiastic about her being so close to the action.

"Remember what we agreed on," he said. "Stay out here behind cover. I don't care what training you have. You're not running out there, guns blazing."

"It's not my first rodeo, sir," she said.

"I understand, but you haven't had a rodeo in over ten years," Rob said.

"What about the gun nest they have set up near the outer perimeter?" Muddler chimed in.

"It's well defended. Walls are sturdy, able to stop a fifty-caliber round. Good place to provide cover fire..." Jean said. Her voice was almost teasing. "Speaking of fifty-cals, they have one up there. That's what I miss the most from the service."

"N. O. NO!" Rob said, his voice expressing a lack of patience. "You understand me?"

Jean sighed sharply. "Yes."

"That AK-47 is for defense. If any of those pricks come out here and makes a move toward you, use it." He adjusted the mic on his helmet. "Everyone ready?"

"*Stroud and I are in position.*"

"Noted. Yellowstone, your team in position?"

"*Affirmative,*" the brute responded.

"Got it. Now that we have a clear line of sight on the facility," he waited a moment to make sure the entire team was listening, "Yellowstone, when I give the word, you and Tire-man prop the accelerators and roll the Jeeps in. Wait for enough of the pricks to draw in on it. After you blast the charges, Yellowstone, you hit the rest with your M60. I'll hit the tents and work my way down to the generator. Steele. Stroud. You see the vehicles there. Don't let any of those pricks make a run for it. We have a friendly in the maintenance shed with at least four guards on it. Muddler will take care of them. Tire-man, Val, and Yellowstone, you guys secure the front lot. Pick out as many of them as you can before they set up a foothold in the research building."

"*Affirmative*," Yellowstone said.

"*Got it, boss,*" Steele said.

Muddler noticed a piercing glare by Rob. "Yes, for the umpteenth time, I get the plan."

"My plans always work for a reason, I make sure everyone knows their jobs," Rob said. "Jean, don't worry about your fiancé. We'll get him out of there."

"Thank you," she replied.

Rob moved to the left, circling the research lab until he was near the back lot. There was a large cement patio leading up the rear entrance. In the clearing between the building and trees were three personnel tents, with at least ten Cobra terrorists moving between them. The tents were lined in a row, separated by about five meters or so. He could see inside one of them through the open flap. It was empty, save for one soldier who moved in and out. The other two were likely empty as well. If not, the upcoming surprise would definitely draw them out.

Up around the right side of the building was the generator. It hummed and crackled. It continued to function, though there were broken components clattering inside of it.

He studied the building itself. It was two stories, with balconies on each side. No doubt the terrorists would use it as a shooting position.

"Yellowstone. Roll them in," he whispered into his microphone.

****

"Got it, boss," Yellowstone replied. He coasted the Jeep out from its hiding place out onto the trail. He could see the camp up ahead. Several soldiers lined the front lot. Tire-man steered the second Jeep out behind him. They stopped the vehicles side by side and disembarked. They placed locks on the steering wheels to keep the Jeeps straight, then propped the accelerators down. Both engines roared to life like mechanical beasts.

Valentine propped the dead terrorists into the driver's seat.

"What's wrong pal? You look pale," he joked, tapping the dead man on the face.

"That's just wrong," Yellowstone said. Valentine tapped on his black heart once more and stepped back. At once, Tire-man and Yellowstone put the two Jeeps in drive. They leapt back as the vehicles raced off, driverless down the road.

They bounced as they tore down the trail, their open doors flapping against their sides. The mercenaries split up and ran into the tree line, with only seconds to take firing position. Yellowstone went to the right and worked his way up to the perimeter. He was only a third of the way when he heard the Jeeps smashing through the perimeter.

****

Rodrigo stepped out through the front entrance, seeing several of his men racing up along the front lawn. The sounds of roaring engines had filled the air, growing louder by the second. Dust billowed up high from the Jeep trail.

The crowd of soldiers broke apart like birds as the two Jeeps raced through the perimeter at top speed. The gates smashed open, the debris striking the station guard in the face. The Jeeps cut through the crowd, rolling over a couple of unlucky terrorists along the way.

Finally, they came to the fork in the path and smashed the parked Jeeps in the front parking lot. Engines imploded, shooting metal fragments throughout the lawn. Soldiers quickly converged on the vehicles and immediately recognized their armed comrades inside.

"What the hell's going on! PAULO!" Rodrigo yelled. He marched toward the lot, stepping over bits of metal.

One of the Cobras pulled the door open and grabbed the driver by the chin, turning his head to face him. He gasped, seeing his dead comrade's face staring back with glazed over eyes.

Overwhelmed by the initial shock, the Cobras never noticed the blocks of C4 falling off of the seat.

****

Yellowstone took position at the tree line. The decoys had smashed into the parking lot and successfully drew away any perimeter guards. He laid down between two trees and propped up his M60. There was a clear line of sight between him and the forty red Cobras that surrounded the vehicles. But before he would open fire…

Yellowstone grabbed the detonator and extended the antennae. "Time to bust open that piñata." He squeezed the button.

The two Jeeps erupted into thunderous fireballs that soared high into the air. Terrorists caught in the blast were launched in the air like meteors. A shockwave rippled through the ground while a huge gust of wind swept through the trees.

Yellowstone followed a group of terrorists with the muzzle of his M60 and squeezed the trigger. The gun kicked as it spat eight-rounds per second. They cut through the targets like invisible razor blades. Blood exploded from entry points as dead terrorists collapsed left and right.

On the other side of the trail, Valentine and Tire-man charged through the perimeter. There were a dozen terrorists on this side of the fork in the driveway, and their attention was diverted between the explosion and machine gun fire.

Valentine was the first to shoot. He aimed high and tapped the trigger. Bullets punched through skull, distending the target's head into a bloated shape. He enjoyed watching the cause-and-effect of headshots. He took down three targets by the time Tire-man opened fire. He aimed traditional center mass. Cobras scattered between the flaming vehicles and fired back. Tire-man fired a three-round, hitting a target just below the neckline. As he went down, the merc aimed past him at another. A red cloud burst from the target's left breast as he spun and fell to the ground.

Valentine picked off two more terrorists then reloaded his weapon. He looked across the lot, seeing white bullet streaks flashing from the tree line into the scattering group of Cobras.

"Can't let him have all of the fun!" he said, tapping Tire-man on the shoulder. They raced behind the smoldering remains of the Jeeps, seeing another group of terrorists ducking behind one of the trucks.

Val could see one of them peeking around the side of the bed near the brake light. He pointed and fired a single shot, exploding the top of the Cobra's head. As his corpse faceplanted, his two comrades attempted to retaliate by opening fire, only to be struck with automatic gunfire by Val and Tire-man.

Rodrigo yelled orders at his men, trying to maintain some degree of method to the defenses. Several terrorists were flooding the lot from the west and south defenses.

"No! No!" he yelled as the men guarding the maintenance shed started to charge the mercenaries at the east lot. They stopped, seeing the commander running toward them.

"Sir! They're attacking!"

"I know they're attacking! I'm telling you to hold position, damn it! They're not only going to attack from that side…" He stumbled backward in surprise as the guard's chest erupted simultaneously to the echo of a sharp crack.

Muddler placed the next target in her sights and fired. The bullet struck the terrorist in the center of his upper back and exited his chest, trailing blood as it continued into the complex. The other two guards were turning to aim into the trees. Luckily, one was directly behind the other.

She placed the front in her crosshairs and squeezed the trigger. The bullet punched through both men. They teetered on their heels and fell in opposite directions.

"Hot damn," Jean commented.

"Never gets old," Muddler replied. They could hear gunfire echoing from the north and west sides as Rob, Steele, and Stroud launched their attacks.

Rob charged inward from the trees, his rifle aimed at the flabbergasted group of terrorists. One turned and saw him just as several rounds cut into his abdomen. The terrorist folded over and hit the ground. Rob raised the rifle to eye level and fired with precision. His shots were well placed and timed, catching each target directly in their center mass. Bodies twisted and fell, their rifles discharging into the air. Rob dashed to the right, evading return fire from two soldiers behind the tents. He moved up and around the other side then placed them in his aim. Skulls burst like egg shells, spraying brain matter on the grass.

He looked up to the balcony. As he predicted, the door opened up and two Cobras stepped out with rifles. They locked eyes with him, realizing he already had them in his aim. They both fired a wild shot, both of which went wide. Rob tapped the trigger repeatedly, punching them repeatedly in the chest until both targets dropped.

Rob replaced the magazine and heard the sound of running footsteps within the facility. He pulled back the cocking lever then switched the weapon to full-auto. The back door flung open and four Cobras spilled out. Rob squeezed the trigger and kept it down. All four figures danced with abrupt lurching motions as they absorbed the full load of the thirty-round magazine.

There was no time to reload. Rob glanced to his left, seeing two more terrorists rushing him from the north corner of the building, AK-47s in hand. He dropped the H&K and drew his sidearm. He fired off several shots as he backtracked, hitting one of them in the neck. The terrorist fell to his knees, his hands clutched around his throat. The other one fired a barrage of bullets, forcing Rob to dive behind the tents.

He army-crawled along the ground, hearing the whistles of several bullets passing within inches of him. The terrorist picked up his dead comrade's rifles and, duel-wielding them, he blasted wildly, hoping for a lucky shot. Rob was pinned, unable to see the terrorist through the tarp. He blindly fired a few return rounds but missed.

The shooting persisted, pinning Rob behind the tent. For the moment, all he could do was wait for the terrorist to reload, and hopefully not land a lucky shot in the meantime.

Steele and Stroud split up and circled the greenhouse, picking off Cobras as they went. Steele hugged the wooden side of the building as he moved up to the front. Steele caught glimpses of fidgety movements around the corner ahead of him. A terrorist waited impatiently, waiting to ambush him when he arrived.

Steele yanked a grenade from his vest, pulled a pin and tossed it like a softball. The grenade rolled up to the corner of the barn and burst, sending a barrage of shrapnel into the bastard waiting.

"HA!" he cheered triumphantly. He moved up, clearing the side of the barn. He glanced down at his kill, seeing the frozen expression of shock on his face. "Dumb son of a..." He heard the whistle of a bullet passing close by. Chunks of polyester exploded in his face, causing him to stumble back in surprise.

Steele quickly backpedaled around the corner of the barn as bullets punched down into the earth, missing him by inches. Behind cover he removed his ball cap. The prick had shot the bill clean off.

"That's not cool," he said, tossing it on the ground. He sprang back out and aimed high. He saw the shooter up on the balcony lining up for another shot at him. Baring teeth, Steele released a spray of gunfire into the terrorist. Glass shattered and blood painted the siding as bullets passed through the target.

Steele turned toward the sound of a struggle. He stepped around the front of the barn and peered through the open doors. There were three dead terrorists. On the ground beyond them was Stroud, locked in a firm grip by a tenacious Cobra. They had disarmed each other of guns and knives, resorting to unarmed combat. Stroud wheezed as he felt his airway cut off. Legs were locked at the ankles behind his back as the terrorist tightened a fierce triangle choke, applying pressure to his neck.

Stroud punched wildly, unable to connect his fists to the target. He glanced over to the doors, seeing Steele watching with an amused look on his face.

Fucking bastard! He's getting a kick out of this!

Stroud held a hand out, beckoning assistance. Steele simply stood there, doing nothing except unpack a stick of gum and stuff it in his mouth. His grin grew wider as Stroud's face turned purple. The hand closed, saved for the middle finger.

Finally, Steele pulled his knife and tossed it to his buddy. Stroud caught it by the handle and shoved the blade into his opponent's ribcage. The Cobra yelled and released his grip. Stroud sucked in a deep breath and plunged the blade into his heart, finishing him off.

The chokehold loosened, allowing Stroud to suck in a breath.

"You...SUCK BALLS!" he rasped at Steele, tossing his knife back. Steele chuckled and sheathed the blade.

"Had a little trouble there, did ya?" he chuckled.

Stroud snatched his submachine gun and inserted a fresh mag.

"I was just waiting to make my move," he remarked.

"I could tell," Steele laughed. They exited the barn and arrived at the northwest corner of the facility. The remaining forces had mostly converged on the front lot where Yellowstone, Tire-man, and Valentine assaulted.

"Let's join the fun," Stroud said, racing into the action. Steele started to follow him but stopped after hearing a few pops from the back of the building. A single Cobra was there, spraying an AK-47 into a tent.

Steele closed the distance and came up behind the shooter. He drew his machete and tapped him on the shoulder. The gunner turned in time to see the blade swinging. It cut his neck down to the bone.

Steele put his boot to the dead terrorist's chest and pulled his machete free. He laughed as Rob stepped out from behind the tent, pistol in hand.

"Jeez, Rob! I should start charging for all these saves!" he joked. "First the cliff edge. Now this guy! I'm starting to think you're losing your touch!"

Rob pointed the pistol toward him. Steele cringed as his boss fired a shot. He glanced back over his shoulder, seeing the terrorist that had come out the back door behind him. The man collapsed onto the ground with a fresh bullet wound to the head.

"You were saying?" Rob retorted. He collected his rifle and loaded a fresh magazine. "Watch that door. Anyone comes out, kill 'em. I'm going around the side."

"Got it," Steele said. He raced to the door and held position. Rob moved along the south side. He could see the maintenance shed. The guards around it had been successfully eliminated. The battle was now concentrated in the front lot, with Cobras retreating from Yellowstone's unrelenting barrage from Yellowstone's M60.

A small group of terrorists retreated back alongside the building. They raised their weapons as they saw Rob standing in their path. His aim was sharper and faster. Fire flickered at his rifle muzzle as he placed a dozen rounds into the group, dropping all three hostiles.

He converged on the gun nest, located several yards to his two o'clock. The gunman aboard unleashed the fifty-cal. on Valentine and Tire-man. The mercenaries barely managed to evade the gunfire, which forced them back behind the tree line.

Rob pulled a grenade and hurled it. The metal ball rolled in the air as it completed its arch, landing right at the Cobra's feet. It burst the instant he looked down at it, blasting the nest into splinters.

Muddler ran ahead to where she could see the front of the building. She could see streaks of gunfire coming from the second-floor windows. Yellowstone moved in from his hiding place and assaulted the northeast section of the lot. He looked like a comic book character, muscled out, holding the M60 with one hand, the ammo chain wrapped around the other. Numerous Cobras fell prey to his wrath. Only the snipers would have a chance at taking him out.

She positioned her rifle and worked her way from left to right. She could see the human shape behind the muzzle flashes. Both disappeared as she squeezed the trigger. She aimed at the center window and fired again. The target spun when hit, blasting several rounds into the ceiling before collapsing.

Muddler adjusted her aim to the final window. The Cobra had discarded his rifle and had pulled two grenades from his belt. She glanced down, realizing Stroud was directly below him, engaged in a firefight with another group.

"Shit!" She aimed quickly and fired. The bullet hit the terrorist in the thigh, blowing his leg off entirely. He fell to the ground, grenades still in hand. They detonated with a tremendous *boom*!

Stroud looked up, seeing fragments of the balcony about to come down on him. His curses were audible as he retreated around the building, narrowly avoiding being crushed by the debris.

Rodrigo sprayed the remaining payload in his magazine, unable to hit the target. The blast from above sent a shockwave down the front of the building, the debris driving him away from the entrance. He saw the rubble that was previously the balcony collapse, with pieces of his comrade raining down with it.

He gazed out, seeing the mercenaries moving in from the trees. Men fell in droves as the big man with the heavy gun blasted them away. There were only a few more setting up a foothold in the building. They wouldn't last long. None of them would.

"The hell with this!" he murmured to himself. He made a mad dash for the north lot. Bullets splintered the building as he went. He cleared the corner, seeing the mercenary with the ugly face. The man moved again, causing Rodrigo to miss yet another shot. He was like a damn mosquito buzzing around his head. Rodrigo didn't waste any more time. He finished the sprint and hopped into one of the Jeeps. Two more soldiers hopped in after him as he started the engine.

Stroud stood up again, his eyes still stinging from dust. He ran his sleeve over them then looked up toward the sound of a roaring engine. Tires screeched as Rodrigo gunned the accelerator.

Stroud squeezed the trigger, spraying several rounds into the engine. Rodrigo cursed and cut the wheel hard to the left, racing the Jeep across the front lawn. Balcony debris went airborne as they smashed through it. Tires crunched rock and gravel as the terrorist smashed through the front porch. Up ahead, another mercenary was stepping out from around the corner. Rodrigo yelled and aimed the engine at him, skidding against the front of the building.

Rob jumped back as the Jeep closed in. It passed by, scraping siding off of the corner of the building as it went. He pointed his rifle and unleashed a barrage of bullets into the side, blowing both tires. He concentrated his aim into the seats, hitting the front passenger as the Jeep plowed through the tree line.

"Secure the building! I'll take care of these guys!" He yelled. With a fresh mag loaded, he charged into the jungle.

Steele entered the rear of the building and passed through a small hallway that led to a locked door. He blasted the handle and kicked it open, seeing two surprised terrorists regrouping in a refrigeration room.

"Knock-knock! Avon calling!"

He double tapped the trigger, blowing their chests wide open.

Up in front, Muddler switched to her submachine gun and joined Yellowstone, Tire-man, and Valentine as they converged on the front entrance. Stroud moved along the wall where the balcony had collapsed, providing cover as they moved in.

Muddler went in first, immediately stepping out as a waiting terrorist opened fire, splintering the doorframe. As soon as the spray stopped, she peeked in again with her weapon pointed and fired a burst of rounds into his neck and jaw, dropping him.

She fired again, hitting another terrorist waiting in the back of the room. Tire-man and Valentine entered the main lobby behind her. They looked up and saw a group of four taking aim from the second-floor atrium. They opened fire in unison, eliminating each of the targets.

The team moved in and secured the lobby. Muddler took the hallway on the left. A Cobra emerged from a room at the end of the hall with a weapon pointed. Muddler fired first, double tapping him in the chest and head. She finished her sweep and secured the hallway.

Muffled gunshots echoed from the deep interior of the building. Muddler raced back to the lobby. A set of double doors in the back of the room opened outward, making way for Steele. On the floor behind him was a freshly dead terrorist.

"No more?"

The team moved upward and secured the bedrooms and lab. No more terrorists awaited them. The building was secured.

Rob quickly found the Jeep, its engine smashed against a tree. Up ahead, Rodrigo and his comrade retreated down a hill, scraping through various obstructions along the way. Sweat poured down Rob's face as he ran after them.

Rodrigo could hear the mercenary on his tail. He could only catch glimpses of him through the terrain. Frustration fried any sense of practical thought. He turned around and fired his pistol into the wall of green. His fellow terrorist stopped, turned, and decided to follow his leader's example. He blasted his AK-47 into the trees.

They waited in silence, unsure whether they hit the target. Smoke twirled from the muzzles of their guns. Rodrigo reloaded his pistol. It was his last magazine. After that, it was just his knife.

His teammate turned, saw something, then yelled.

Rob opened fire, nearly cutting him in half down the middle. Rodrigo shot wildly and ran again. Rob aimed for him and squeezed the trigger. *Click*.

"Figures," he muttered. He ran after the target, drawing his pistol from his hip.

Rodrigo grimaced as he cut through a series of thick bushes. Branches slapped him in the face as if the jungle itself was punishing him for his sins. He passed through about fifty yards before his foot snagged on something on the ground, causing him to sprawl on his belly. His pistol bounced off his hand into the canvas.

Running footsteps were closing in behind him. Rodrigo pulled his knife and stood up, then found a thick tree to hide behind.

Rob heard his movements. He arrived and saw the bends in the grass where the target had fallen. He realized there were no more sounds of flight. The target was hiding around here somewhere.

He gripped his firearm and explored the area, watching down the sights. He checked some nearby bushes to see if Rodrigo was hiding there. Nothing.

The terrorist peeked around the tree. The mercenary's back was turned. Now was the time to strike! He sprang from his hiding place and with a few large strides, he closed in on the enemy.

Rob whirled around. The blade slashed, nicking his wrist and forcing the pistol away from his grasp. Rob raised his hands defensively and strode backward, dodging a second slash.

The two men circled each other. Rodrigo waved the knife then charged. He thrust the weapon forward. Rob snatched his wrist, stopping the blade from reaching his stomach. Rotating his hands clockwise, he twisted Rodrigo's outstretched arm, nearly bending it out of proportion. Rodrigo was forced to go with the motion or suffer a broken limb. Rob rotated to the right, and in a whipping motion, he swung his enemy by the arm like a baseball bat. Rodrigo flipped head over heels as he was thrown. He smacked into a tree, blowing the air from his lungs before falling to the dirt.

Adrenaline surged through his veins. His temper flared, causing him to bare bloodied teeth. He shot to his feet, still holding the knife, and charged again. He slashed, missing Rob by inches. Frustrated, he moved in and slashed a second time.

Once again, Rob caught him by the wrist. This time, he used the momentum to twist Rodrigo's body completely around, locking his arm up over his shoulder. His elbow was now pointed toward the sky, his hand and knife locked down behind his shoulder blade. His back arched, his knees buckling. Rodrigo was barely able to stand upright, much less break out of the hold. Nerves in his arm and shoulder lit up like fireworks as Rob pried the knife from his hand. He yanked down hard on his arm, over-extending Rodrigo's arched posture and threw him down on his back.

The terrorist scurried backward on all fours then stood up. The mercenary held his knife up, taunting him with it. He tossed it up playfully, watching it twirl like a baton before catching it. Rodrigo seethed. It was evident he would not defeat the merc in close quarters. And he would not outrun him. On top of that, it would be a cold day in hell before he allowed himself to be captured. That left one remaining option. He pulled a grenade from his vest and pulled the pin.

Rob saw the lever fall free, meaning the fuse was ignited. Rodrigo started to charge in a suicide bombing attempt.

With a flicking motion of his wrist, he flung the knife. The blade coursed through the air like a bullet, plunging deep through Rodrigo's left eye. He pitched backward and hit the ground. The grenade rolled from his hand and detonated, splurging his body.

"Explosive occurrences tend to happen if you can't hold your wad," Rob remarked.

He collected his weapons and started back toward the facility.

CHAPTER 13

"Hang on! We'll get you out!" Jean called to Trevor. She was digging through the pockets of the dead guards around the shed, unable to find the key to the lock. She could hear Trevor Malloy shrieking in pain.

"Fuck! Hurry! They're all over the place!" he cried. Jean growled in frustration, finding nothing but cigarettes in the terrorists' pockets.

"Get out of the way," Steele ordered. She stepped back, seeing the mercenary drawing his machete. He slammed its handle hard on the lock. He struck repeatedly until the shackle busted in two. Jean yanked it free and pulled the door open. Trevor came sprinting out, slapping his own face to get the ants off of him. He had torn his shirt off and whipped it at his body, knocking away the little pests. His skin was red and blistered, his hair and beard frizzled.

Jean rushed to his side as he collapsed on the ground. His thigh was even more swollen than before. The pant leg around it was torn, revealing a blood-soaked bandage that was covered in ants. The skin was red with infection. Trevor writhed while clawing at his own face. Little black spots scurried over his skin, sinking their little mandibles deep inside. She took off her jean jacket and brushed it over his skin to sweep them off.

Rob stepped out from the jungle. He saw Tire-man standing by the generator, trying to see if he could patch up the damage. Standing next to him was Stroud. He was rubbing his fingers over his bruised neck.

"Report," Rob demanded.

"We checked the bodies. Isagana's not here and there's no sign of Bischoff," Stroud answered.

"Damn," Rob said. "I was hoping we'd catch them after they returned."

"You think we should wait here and set up an ambush?" Stroud asked. Rob looked up, seeing the trails of smoke lifting high above the tree line.

"Not here," Rob said. "Even if they didn't hear the explosions, they undoubtedly will notice that. The path inland leads to higher elevation. This dust cloud could be seen for a couple miles."

"Oh, shit, you're right," Stroud said. "What do you think we should do? Go after him?"

Rob glanced at the hostages by the shed.

"I'm trying to decide," he said. "I don't want to take them along into another firefight. At the same time, I'm not comfortable leaving them here either."

"We can't wait too long," Tire-man said. "They still have Dr. Bischoff."

"I'm well aware," Rob said.

Steele kneeled down and helped Jean to lift Trevor to his feet.

"Let's get him to the bathroom. We need to get these clothes off and rinse him off. The water should still work...I hope," she said.

"Don't expect me to be there for that," Steele quipped.

"I'd offer to get the door, but..." Valentine remarked, looking at the busted front entrance. Yellowstone stepped out, dragging two Cobra bodies over his shoulder. He stood aside, making way for the scientists and Steele.

Muddler was already halfway up the stairs when she saw them coming. There was nothing she could do to assist other than open the bathroom door for them.

"Thank you," Jean said as she and Steele took Trevor inside. She sat Trevor on the toilet seat and twisted the shower knob. Water sprayed from the faucet, much to her relief. "Oh, thank God."

"Who the hell are these guys?" Trevor said, pinching the bugs off of his face.

"Your new best friends," Steele answered. He stepped out and shut the door behind him. He stepped into the second-floor lobby, seeing Muddler approaching the corner on the opposite side. Directly in front of her was the lab. She tugged on the handle. To her surprise, the door was unlocked. The lab itself was chilly, which felt good compared to the hot air outside.

Steele followed her in, curious to see what experiments were taking place. They saw a large bright room with a large rectangular lab table running down the center. Everywhere they looked was equipment, pipes, wires, monitors, scopes, x-ray machines and other machines that neither mercenary knew what purpose they served.

"Where's the big slab with *Frankenstein's Monster?*" Steele joked. Muddler ignored him and stepped further inside. To the right of the room was a row of enormous glass tubes, attached in large bulky machines. Each contained IV lines, a heartrate monitor, and other devices. They looked like a cross between medical equipment and a hyper-sleep chamber from a science fiction movie. Yet, though they were fairly large, they were too small for a human. A baby perhaps. A small child at most.

Steele eyeballed a metal door on the opposite side of the room. He peered through the circular window, seeing a nearly empty chamber. In the center of it was a large glass cube. Next to the door were silver suits resembling something a hazmat team would wear. Whatever the room was, his mind warned him it was best to keep that door shut. Yet, he found himself staring at that weird box.

It was clear, with a black vial in the middle and a sterilized syringe. The box was almost perfectly sealed. There were two gloves inserted, attached to armholes at the front of the bizarre cube. From what he could see, those gloves were made of a thick rubber.

"Radioactive isotope?" he asked himself.

"What?" Muddler asked.

"Nothing," he said and stepped away from the door. He walked along the table, glancing at the microscopes and syringes. There was another machine with a glass tube at the center of the lab table. The monitors were still on, though reading flatlines. He could see the edge of the glass tube, which faced the opposite side. However, he could tell that something was inside. He stepped around the back of the table and came back along the opposite side. At the same time, Muddler approached to take a look at the tube.

They gazed at the hideous malformed creature inside. It was the size of a three-month old infant. Reptilian claws were curled under bulky human-like arms. Its entire body was covered in rigid scales, dark grey in color. Steele found himself staring at the elongated crocodile snout protruding from the ape-like head. The eyes were open, almost like those of a cat.

"Hoooooly SHIT!" he exclaimed.

Valentine and Yellowstone proceeded on loading the bodies onto one of the trucks, clearing the front and side lot. As they did, Rob observed the north lot. There were two Jeeps and a cargo truck remaining in addition to the pickup truck that Valentine drove. The Jeeps had been heavily damaged in the firefight. The truck, though having suffered some damage from stray bullets, appeared to be in relatively good condition.

"Get Tire-man come and give this truck a look-over," Rob told Stroud.

"We going after 'em?" Stroud asked.

"Hopefully not," Rob said. "We're gonna take the trail out for about a mile and set a trap. If they do return, they'll be planning to launch an attack here at the facility. Unless we ambush them along the way."

Steele stepped out onto the front patio and shouted at him.

"Hey, Rob! You might wanna check this out!"

Rob could sense the tension in his voice.

"Keep watch," he ordered to Stroud as he joined Steele at the front entrance. He followed him up the stairs and into the cool lab. Muddler was still staring at the strange creature in the tube, as though hypnotized by it.

"Did the government guys mention *this?!*" Steele said, pointing his finger at it. Rob gazed at the abomination inside. Those crocodilian jaws were gaped open, the creature itself in a twisted pose.

"No. They did not."

The cold water hit like an electric shock, causing Trevor to shiver. It did, however, feel refreshing after being stuck in that dirty unfinished shed. The ants were off of him now and washing down the drain. He ran his fingers through his hair, shaking any stragglers loose.

Jean could tell he was still in immense pain. The Cobras had denied any pain medication for his leg, and barely supplied him sufficient antibiotics. On top of that, he clearly needed to see a dentist for his cracked tooth. The whole left side of his jaw was rounded, now covered in bite marks from those ants.

"Let me help," she said. She wrapped a towel around him and guided him onto the toilet seat. He leaned against her and hobbled on his good leg.

"Where's Bischoff?" he asked.

"He's still out there. With Isagana," Jean said. Trevor perked up.

"Wait? These guys didn't intercept him?"

"No," she said. She removed the old gauze, wincing at the gaping bullet wound. As she feared, it had been reopened. She placed some fresh gauze on it then taped it up. Trevor swallowed hard as she held up a syringe full of antibiotics. He hated needles and this one looked as menacing as ever. He turned to his side and winced as she stuck it in his buttocks.

Jean thought about what the mercenaries said about the harbor. "There's something weird going on. I say it's time we got off this island."

"What about the Doc?" Trevor said, gritting teeth as she removed the needle. He took a breath and sat straight. "We can't leave without him."

There was a heavy knock on the door. Trevor made sure he was properly covered up with the towel before Jean opened it a crack. It was Rob on the other side, his face looking inquisitive.

"Doctor, do you have a moment?"

Jean glanced back at Trevor.

"I'm good," he said. "You go ahead and see what he needs. I can dress myself."

Jean left the bathroom and followed Rob across the lobby into the lab. She was relieved to find that the refrigeration units were still functional, keeping the equipment and test subjects properly stored. Rob moved to the large incubation tube at the center of the table and pointed to the occupant inside.

"Care to explain what you guys were working on in here?" Rob said. Muddler and Steele stood by him, both staring at the bizarre ape-lizard thing. Muddler almost looked ill from its disgusting features, yet somehow couldn't look away.

"It was not what we came to this island to do," Jean said.

"I figure this was Isagana's plan," Rob said. "Then again, he knew you and Dr. Bischoff were the people to do the job. What were you trying to do on this island?"

"We were cross-breeding plant species," Jean explained. "See, Dr. Bischoff was developing a method for growing food in barren areas. For instance, he was combining wheat with desert cactus cells. This new wheat would be grown out in the desert."

"You were combining cells?" Muddler clarified. Jean nodded.

"Long story short, Isagana came to the island and took over the place, killed our staff, and forced us to work," Jean said. "Isagana wanted Bischoff's research to develop bio-weapons for his sick agenda. He forced us to use our research to combine the cells of various species of animals."

"For what? Was he expecting to use them as his attack dogs?" Steele asked.

"For starters," Jean said. "It gets sicker than that. What he REALLY wanted to do was combine human DNA with other creatures. Essentially, he wanted to develop a new breed of hybrid super soldiers."

Rob shook his head in disgust.

"He was always a sick bastard."

"This one is dead," Muddler pointed out. "Have any test subjects survived the process?"

"No," Jean answered. "Part of the problem is the growth supplement we have supplied to them. Isagana didn't have the patience for a typical incubation period, so he made us use our radioactive isotope to accelerate the growth."

"Oh, nice thinking on his part. *NOTHING* could go wrong with that!" Steele remarked.

"That's what we tried to explain to him. He didn't care," Jean said. "The CV-30 isotope was too much for their little bodies. The cells were mutating too fast. In addition, they were growing too fast for their development to keep up. Their organs were under-developing, which resulted in us losing each one."

"Probably would've gotten cancer anyway," Steele remarked.

"How many hybrids have you tried?" Muddler asked, her voice sounding awed.

"A lot," Jean said. "This thing here, a bird-reptile crossover, a couple of fish species, some other reptilian ones, insect and—"

"What happens to the test subjects?" Rob asked.

"There's a ridge near the center of the island," Jean said. "It's called Odessa Ridge. That's where the Red Cobras have been going to discard the dead specimens…and the bodies of our colleagues. Isagana thought you guys parachuted into the island center because a patrol hadn't returned from the Ridge. He went to check it out. Took Bischoff as a hostage."

"Shit," Rob said. He stepped out of the lab and rested on the atrium rail. Muddler followed him out, immediately feeling the humid air seeping through the various breaches in the building.

"We gonna go after him?" she asked.

"Hell, I say we get the hell out of here," Steele said. "Something weird is going on here on this island."

"We can't leave without Dr. Bischoff," Rob said. Steele bit his lip.

"Hey, Rob, I want to kill that Isagana bastard as much as you do—"

"I couldn't care less about that," Rob interrupted. "For now, at least. But we can't leave a hostage behind. Besides, the plane won't return unless we finish the job."

Steele backed up, raising his hands in defeat.

"Okay. Then what's the plan?"

"Jean, how many men went with Isagana?" Rob asked. The doctor joined them in the lobby.

"I think eight," she said. "I'm not completely sure. My group left before his. Considering the number of people still here, it had to be a small group."

"He's likely to return, though I think he suspects something's gone wrong here," Rob said. "I'm gonna go out on the north route with Valentine, Yellowstone, and Tire-man. Muddler, you, Steele, and Stroud cover the east route. Set up a trap a mile out to ambush them should they come in from that way. Jean, you can handle a weapon. Wait here with Dr. Malloy until we're finished. I doubt they'll get past us, but if they do, you'll know what to do."

"You got it," she responded, thumbing the strap of her AK-47.

CHAPTER 14

It had been several hours. Rob and his team were as still as statues as they waited for the truck to return. The smell of pesticides had filled their nostrils, causing an annoying burning sensation in their throats. Jean wasn't kidding when she mentioned that they have been spraying incessantly. Whatever the terrorists have been spraying must have worked because Rob hadn't seen a single insect around the compound so far.

What wasn't working was this plan. So far, Isagana had not returned. At the start of each hour, Rob had checked in with Muddler's team, who had reported similar progress.

"They should've been here by now," Tire-man said. He was crouched five feet to Rob's right, almost invisible beneath the huge bush leaves.

"I know," Rob whispered.

"We have limited daylight left," Tire-man reminded him.

"I'm aware," Rob said.

"You think he went to the coast?"

"It's possible," Rob responded. "He won't get any ride and he has no radio to reach out." Several more minutes passed. It was the start of the next hour. Rob raised his radio to his lips. "Any updates?"

"*Nothing*." Muddler's voice was a ghostly whisper. Rob sucked in a deep breath, ignoring the burning stench of the pesticide. He shook his head in defeat.

"Report back to the compound," he ordered. He and Tire-man stood up and stepped onto the trail. Yellowstone and Valentine emerged from the other side.

"Change of plan, Boss?" the heavy gunner asked.

"Yes. We're going in after them," Rob said. "Tire-man, you're driving."

79

"I don't know, Boss. Putting an Asian behind the wheel is like putting a bull in a china factory," Valentine said.

"Funny," the North Korean said.

"Hang on! I gotta take a leak!" Yellowstone said. He turned to face the jungle.

"Oh jeez," Rob said. He turned his back, listening to Yellowstone's stream tapping against the bush leaves.

****

The team regrouped at the north lot. Tire-man and Yellowstone fueled the truck while the other mercenaries boarded the compartment.

"What do you want to do about them?" Steele asked, tilting his head over at Jean and Trevor, who were at the front porch. Trevor leaned on his crutch, his body still shaking from exhaustion. Jean had her rifle slung over her shoulder. Her arms were crossed. She was obviously not keen on being left here at the compound.

Rob hated crossroad decisions like this. He hated the idea of taking them along into a possible firefight. On the other hand, he wasn't keen on splitting up his team to keep them guarded. Going further into the thick jungle would likely interfere with radio communications.

"You're not seriously expecting us to wait here, are you?" Jean said.

"Won't your plane pick us up?" Trevor asked.

"At this point, it'll be a couple of hours at least before they would arrive," Rob explained. "They're trying to keep out of U.S. Naval waters. Remember, we're not *really* here."

"By the time they'd get here we'd lose our daylight," Muddler added.

"Then we're coming along," Jean demanded. Rob groaned audibly. He glanced at the complex, seeing the aftermath of their firefight. Almost all of the Red Cobras had been taken care of, except for one small band led by the priority target. The feeling of being so close, yet so far from completing the mission was extremely aggravating.

"I can stay with them," Muddler said.

"No," Rob said. "I don't like the idea of splitting up. This isn't the same as setting up ambushes a mile from each other." He thought for a moment. Unfortunately, the civilians would probably be safer tagging along than they would be waiting here. "Alright, fine. You can come with us. But you'll follow my instructions and don't be venturing off if we come to any stops. Any shooting happens, you keep behind cover and only move when I tell you to. Understood?"

"Yes," Trevor and Jean spoke at once.

"Good. Let's get on board," Rob said. The team boarded the back of the truck and took their seats while Rob and Tire-man sat up front. The engine roared and black exhaust billowed from the pipe. The tires spun, carrying the team deep into the trail.

Rob watched as they slipped into the shade provided by the canopy. The sun had begun its descent to the west. Hopefully they would find Isagana before dark, kill him, and get off this accursed island.

Something in him knew it wasn't gonna be that simple.

CHAPTER 15

Even at thirty miles an hour, the truck bumped heavily as though it was driving over rocks. The dirt trail was still solid and uneven. The group that had cleared it out had done a rush-job at best.

There were several bends in the trail to swerve around the trees. Tire-man was constantly forced to slow to a near-stop as he approached each one. He almost wished the Jeeps had been in reasonable condition, as they would've been easier to drive on this narrow path. It was certainly not designed for the passage of large trucks.

The truck hit another bump, rocking the mercenaries in their seats.

"Damn," Rob muttered. The sliding panel opened behind him. He could see Valentine's face peering through at him from the other side.

"Hey, I warned you about letting Asians drive," he joked. Tire-man deliberately slammed on the brakes, causing Valentine to fall forward and bump his head into the frame. "FUCK!"

Rob failed to suppress a much-needed laugh. Valentine continued muttering various curse words as he returned to his seat. Tire-man kept an eye back through the panel, watching his teammate starting to sit down. He hit the accelerator, nearly making Valentine fall to the floor.

"HEY!" he yelled. The group laughed at his misery.

"Don't pick a fight you can't win," Stroud said.

"You suck," Valentine snapped.

"God, I feel like I'm on the school bus headed for Fifth Grade," Trevor Malloy said. He chuckled at his own joke, only to wince in pain. He put a hand to his jaw, then clutched his leg as the truck shook again. His leg hurt so bad he felt it would fall off any moment.

"Hiding a football somewhere in that thigh?" Steele said, staring at the injury.

"Might as well be," Trevor groaned. "I've been getting my ass kicked since day one of these fuckers coming here."

"Is that part of that Fifth Grade flashback?" Stroud joked. Trevor glared at him, pretending to be offended, then chuckled at the joke.

"I guess the boot fits. I was always the nerd. Nerds are always getting chased on the playground."

"Not her," Muddler said. She leaned in toward Jean and gave her a high-five.

"Thought they were gonna kiss for a sec," Valentine remarked, sporting a wide grin. He noticed a look of disgust from Jean.

"Don't mind him," Yellowstone said. "He's the result of Scotch and an immigration scam."

"Oh! Thought it was inbreeding," Jean retorted.

"Well holy goddamn!" Valentine said, absorbing the verbal punishment.

"Behave back there," Rob called back. He checked his watch. It was late afternoon by now. At this pace it would take the rest of the day to continue through the trail and back to the harbor.

The terrain only got worse as the trail led to higher elevation. The truck jolted as it hit various indentations in the ground. Grass and weeds were already trying to reclaim the thin clearing. Large bushes beginning to take form. The construction crew had not bothered to spray anything to prevent growth.

Tire-man slowed the truck as they came around another bend. The path straightened for several hundred feet. But there was something up ahead, partially blocking it.

"Whoa," he muttered. Rob saw the Dodge pickup truck up ahead. It was on its side, the nearby tree line in tatters.

"What the hell did this?" he said. Tire-man brought the truck to a stop. Rob stepped out and inspected the crash. The mercenaries filed out of the truck. Jean followed them, immediately noticing Rob's look of disapproval. "Didn't I tell you to wait in there?!"

"This is the truck that delivered the last load of failed experiments to the ridge," Jean pointed out.

"And look at this," Steele said. He was pointing to tire marks in the dirt. There were empty cartridges all over the ground around it, along with a few faint footprints. "Something took place here."

Rob looked at the tracks. "These aren't from some Jeep. They're from a heavier vehicle. Doctor, did Isagana have another truck like this one?"

"Yes," she answered. "It was there when Paulo took me up to the harbor. He must've taken it."

"Something drove them off in a hurry," Yellowstone said.

"Maybe it was the *Hulk*," Stroud said, looking at the damage to the pickup. Rob gave it a closer look. First, he observed the strange cavity in the side then the shards of broken glass.

"This blood is almost a day old," he said. He turned around and followed the tire tracks up around the next bend. The bend led to another, where the tracks continued on to a hole in the forest line. The brush had been flattened, with slivers of paint and metal littering the ground where the truck had passed between two trees.

The truck itself wasn't there. Though it had plowed deep into the woods, it had backed out and continued on.

"Odd that they didn't return to the complex," Steele said. Rob didn't respond. He was looking at the ground again, noticing odd groves in the dirt. Steele saw them too. They were everywhere, each a meter long and a couple inches deep. They were just like the markings they had seen in the construction site, each two-in-a-row, as if a giant two-pronged pitchfork had been raked several times over.

There were traces of leaked oil and washer fluid in the dirt, along with shards of broken glass and pieces of tire rubber.

"They couldn't have gone far," Rob said.

"Should we keep going?" Steele said.

"We don't have a choice," Rob said.

****

All sense of levity was gone as the team boarded the truck again. Though Rob wouldn't show it, the team could tell he was getting increasingly nervous. Something strange was occurring on this island and he didn't know what.

Tire-man carefully maneuvered the truck around the next bend and followed the tracks. Rob kept his fingers wrapped tightly around his rifle. It took strong discipline to keep his finger off the trigger. Watching the jungle passing by his window, he could feel himself growing jumpy. Something large had knocked over that pickup truck and had chased Isagana's truck inland. Now he didn't even feel safe in this heavy military vehicle.

Tire-man put additional pressure on the accelerator to get the truck up a small hill. Rob stuck his head out of the window to get a better look at the dirt. The globs of oil were thicker here. Isagana had clearly been this way recently.

The trail curved again at the top of the hill. Tire-man gulped as he tapped on the brakes to prevent them from going off the path. He gulped again as he steered to the other side of the bend, which led to the edge of a wood bridge over what appeared to be a large pond.

"Whoa!" he said, bringing the truck to a full stop.

"Now what?" Steele called from the back.

Rob shouldered his rifle and disembarked. He approached the edge of the pond and looked down. There was no bottom. The walls seemed to go straight down forever. This was no pond, it was a chasm that had filled with water, probably years ago.

The forest around it was extremely thick, with trees crowding so close together that the construction crew must've decided it was easier to build a bridge over the chasm.

The body of water around the platform was still and deep. If it were any longer, it'd be a lake. It was deep enough to submerge the truck entirely. Rob could see several fractures in the support beams. Something had weakened the structure drastically. There were traces of oil over the incline, confirming that Isagana had come through this way. There were a few cracks in the platform itself along with numerous grooves that splintered the wood.

"You think it's sturdy enough for our truck?" Tire-man asked. Rob took a few steps onto the bridge. It seemed sturdy enough but then again there was a vast difference between supporting his weight and the weight of a six-ton vehicle.

"Everyone get out," Rob said.

Tire-man stuck his head out of the window. "What?"

"Do I really have to repeat myself?"

Tire-man sucked in a deep breath and disembarked. The rest of the team exited the truck behind him, with Valentine and Steele supported Trevor. Rob came up to the driver's seat, taking Tire-man's place at the wheel.

"You sure you wanna take that thing across?" Steele said, nervously looking at the bridge.

"I can swim if it gives. Not like it's a raging river," Rob said. "But I don't want it going down with all of us inside of it. Especially not him." Rob pointed at the injured Trevor Malloy.

He slammed the door shut and slowly steered the vehicle close to the edge of the bridge. He cringed at the sound of creaking of wood as the truck came up along the incline. There was a mild juddering underneath him. The truck came up onto the structure and slowly moved forward. Each beam trembled under the weight. Clearly it was made for smaller vehicles in mind.

Rob eased on the accelerator, barely putting the truck over coasting speed. The beams continued to creak under the tires. However, the bridge held. Rob breathed a sigh of relief as the truck cleared the opposite side onto dry land. He parked the truck and waved to the others. The team hustled to the bridge, with Valentine and Steele lifting Trevor completely off the ground and carrying him to the truck.

Rob moved aside for Tire-man to take the wheel. Once the team was loaded inside, the North Korean hit the pedal. The truck rocked, passing over a shabby, unmaintained trail.

****

The trail of motor oil led them past a juncture, where the trail intersected with another that led to a route to the harbor. Tire-man drove another hundred yards, following the tire marks up ahead.

"There it is," Rob said.

The cargo truck was empty. Huge flaps of metal had been torn from the sidings as though it had been surgically opened up. The engine had been completely smashed, with thick globs of motor oil pooling underneath it. The engine was still smoking, though it had cooled significantly. And like at the start of the oil trail, the ground was completely marked up with enormous grooves.

There was no sign of Isagana or anyone else in the vehicle.

"Son of a bitch," Rob muttered, frustrated. Something on the ground caught his eye. He stepped out of the truck and knelt down. There were a dozen oddly shaped shards, all black and strangely shaped. They reminded him of fragments of egg shell, despite being extremely large. He picked one up. The texture was rough and the underside contained a yellow gooey substance. "What the hell is going on?"

"I saw something like those down at the harbor," Tire-man said. "They were in the water. One piece had bullet holes in it."

"Where to now?" Tire-man asked. "Should we take the other route? Head down to the beach?"

Rob shook his head. "Jean? How far is it to the ridge?"

"About two miles," she answered.

"It's at least eight or nine to the harbor," Trevor added. Rob glanced at the markings on the ground, which appeared to continue up the current path. Whatever they were, they were related to Isagana's whereabouts.

"Let's check the Ridge first," Rob said. "I don't feel like traveling up here more than once in case he's not anywhere else."

"Sooner we find the doctor and get out of here, the better," Steele said.

CHAPTER 16

They drove over rocky hills and gravelly earth until the path concluded at a large mountainous region. Rob stared up at the steep wall of rock that poked high to the sky. It was just one segment of a huge mountain that gave the island its name. The ridge extended from the end of the wall and stretched out for a hundred yards or more. Odessa Ridge was nothing more than a shallow crevice in the center of the island. Jean Kyunghee had suspected it to be part of a fault line that ran through the island. She had a theory that it had originally been an extension of the mountain itself until an earthquake broke it apart. Whatever the case was, the region was hollow, much like the mountain itself.

The jungle here was far more spacious, with only a few trees near the mountain. The ground was made of solid rock, not apposite for the growth of most plants. All around the base of the mountain, the ground was littered with metal scraps and various other remains. Amongst them were strips of clothing, pieces of metal and glass, weapons, and various other scraps. Rob immediately noticed the abandoned bulldozer and crane parked a hundred feet from the steep ledge of Odessa Ridge. It wasn't as deep as he expected; maybe thirty or forty feet. The earth leading up to the crevice had been scraped up, likely from the bulldozer to dump sediment on the dead.

"Stop here," Rob said. Tire-man pulled the truck over near the tree line. Rob stepped out and gazed at the enormous rock wall. The mercenaries disembarked and fanned out, weapons raised for firing.

Steele and Stroud were the first to move to the ledge. "Take a look at that!" one of them said. Rob and Muddler joined them and gazed down at the crevice. The sediment below looked as though it had been…dug out. Mounds of brown dirt and grey rock had been mixed about as though the entire pit had been put through a blender. Yet, there was nothing visible below. There were no bodies, human or otherwise. The only thing that wasn't a natural part of the earth were the glass tubes that contained their failed experiments. The glass had been shattered, the metal components ripped apart.

"Where are the experiments?" Jean said.

"Probably mixed somewhere in the ground," Stroud remarked. "I imagine those tubes would shatter once dropped."

"Yeah, except that glass around those tubes are supposed to be bullet proof. Those bulldozers would have to drop boulders on them to bust them open."

"Holy shit…was *that* always there?" Steele said, pointing his rifle to the side where the crevice connected with the mountain. The team quickly gathered, seeing an enormous hole in the base of the rock. It was at least twenty feet in width. Several tons of sediment were piled up around the mouth of the opening, which partially obscured their view of it.

"No…that was not there," Jean said. Much of it appeared to have been dug out within the past month. Rob glanced around. There didn't appear to be any digging equipment for this kind of job. "Wait a minute…" she knelt down for a closer look. There was something mixed in with the pile of soot. She noticed the white rounded face looking back at her. Two large sockets were filled with dirt. "Oh, GOD!" she muttered, realizing she was looking at a human skull.

Trevor stuck his head out, hearing his fiancée's sounds of distress. He gazed up the side of the mountain, noticing odd holes in the rock. They were scattered all over, like pores. And like the cave, they weren't there before.

"That's it. We're leaving," Rob said.

"We can't go!" Trevor called out. "We HAVE to find Bischoff!"

"Listen, Dr. Malloy, there's something going on here and we're not prepared to handle it," Valentine said.

"The plane won't come back until we have something to tell them," Muddler said.

"We'll just tell them Isagana's dead!" Steele snapped.

"You mean lie?"

"It might not be a lie," Steele said, pointing at the bones.

"Yeah? And if he's still alive and manages to conduct another bombing?" Muddler said. "Who do you'll think will take the fall for that?"

"Guys?" Tire-man interrupted. Nobody listened.

"I'd rather deal with that than whatever's killing everybody on this island!" Valentine argued.

"GUYS!" Tire-man yelled this time.

"Knock it off!" Rob ordered. His voice boomed over the group, who immediately ceased their argument. Rob heard Tire-man yell but couldn't see him.

"Over here," Jean said. She pointed down over the edge of the crevice. Rob approached the ledge and looked down. Tire-man had climbed down the wall. It wasn't steep and had several points to grab on to. He worked his way down with relative ease, quickly touching the bottom.

"What are you doing?" Rob called down to him.

"I see something," Tire-man answered. He moved over the loose mounds of soil toward the edge of the cliff.

"Shit," Rob muttered. He turned to face the team. "Steele, Valentine, you're with me." The team branched out while Rob initiated the climb. It was a fairly simple process, helped by a steady incline of the crevice wall. He reached the bottom then approached the mouth of the cave. Tire-man shined a flashlight into the gullet of the mountain.

"What is it?" Steele asked. Tire-man took several steps in, stopping where the sunlight stopped. There was a gaping hole on the ground near the cave wall. The hole was roughly six feet wide with several small scratches in the soil around it. Tire-man aimed his flashlight deep into the hole. The white light stretched as far as it could go, illuminating the dark soil of the tunnel walls. The tunnel stretched down about sixty feet or so before it curved away out of sight, leading to an unknown destination deep below.

"That's not a natural formation," Steele said.

Rob attached his flashlight to his rifle barrel and panned it left and right. There were other such holes in the cave walls. Some were high, while others were nearer to the ground.

The light crossed over one of the holes, illuminating something in the dirt. Noticing the red color, Rob thought it was blood. A more concentrated look made him realize it was not fluid, but fabric material. A bandana! He stepped in and picked it up, then looked at his men.

He recalled the picture given to him by the man in black. It was the same bandanna that Dr. Bischoff wore.

"Shit," Steele said. "He's in here somewhere."

"Let's go a little further in," Rob said.

Jean waited with Trevor by the truck. She was staring at the ground, worried about Dr. Bischoff. The mercenaries fanned out, none of them saying a word as they waited for Rob and the others to finish inspecting the cave. Yellowstone waited by the ledge, keeping his M60 pointed in case any surprises should emerge. As he stood guard, he watched as

Stroud initiated a quick climb down into the crevice. The scar-faced mercenary reached the bottom and inspected the glass containers in the soil.

"What do you see?" Yellowstone called down to him. Stroud didn't answer right away. He nudged a glass tube with his boot, noticing dry blood from whatever sick experiment was inside of it.

"Watch out," Trevor warned her. Jean looked down and saw the six-inch long scorpion approaching her foot. She kicked it away, watching it flail as it rolled into the jungle.

Muddler stood close by the truck, watching the trees. As before, there was hardly a sound coming from the jungle. It was as though it had been stripped of all life. Jean noticed it too. While working as a hostage, she hardly spent any quality time outside. But she recalled how the jungle was before the Red Cobras took over. It was vibrant, with birds, lizards, mammals, and monkeys seen at every turn. Now, there was nothing.

"What the hell was in here?" Stroud interrupted the silence. He was climbing up the side of the crevice after picking something off the ground. Jean approached, realizing he was holding the base of a test tube.

"It's the smaller version of the artificial womb. This one in particular was for nurturing eggs," she answered. Stroud noticed the shakiness in her voice. There was a realization in her facial expression. Trevor hobbled out of the truck, leaning on his crutch as he joined her.

Jean took the container from Stroud and examined it. The label was still inscribed on the metal base. *Trial 3-2.* Inside were decomposing fragments of what had been the egg sack inside of it. The tube was intact, save for a single hole in the side.

"No…" she muttered. "It can't be alive…"

"We ran the tests," Trevor said. His voice sounded as though he was trying to convince *himself* other than anyone else. "It was flatlined."

"How many times did you check?" Jean asked.

"Just once. Isagana got angry and hauled it away before I could do anything else."

"What?" Stroud asked, his gaze narrowing.

"What was in that? What did Isagana make you create?" Muddler asked. Jean couldn't answer. She was struggling with comprehending the possibility. She and Trevor shared a horrified stare, before both noticing the local species of scorpion reemerging from the tree line.

Rob took a few steps deeper until he was consumed by the darkness of the cave. The flashlight glistened over a silky substance that had been caked all over the walls. The cave itself seemed to stretch forever into the mountain with no end in sight. He took each step slowly, panning his light on a row of dried skeletons along the right side.

Rob stopped. There was something up ahead, down on the left corner. Rob flipped the lever on his rifle, switching to full-auto, then aimed his flashlight.

He saw shreds of military-style clothing strewn about over a large pool of blood. The blood streamed from the body of a Red Cobra terrorist. The stomach had been torn completely open, the flesh stripped off the face. Ribs protruded upward, some of them snapped in two, with little meat remaining.

Just a few feet beyond it was another body in similar condition. The bones had snapped, the arms and head torn completely free. The wall behind the bodies was splattered with blood.

"Jesus," Steele muttered, seeing the carnage. He stopped and pointed his gun, noticing the feet were moving slightly. Something was nudging the body.

"Hold up..." Rob warned. The three of them fanned out. The body nudged again. Warm blood splashed their boots. It was as though the body was exploding from the inside.

A series of tiny hisses pierced the air. Spider-like legs flickered from the body cavity.

"The hell is that?" Valentine said, disgusted.

Between those legs was a segmented body, trailing a curved tail behind it. Two pincers clasped in front of its face. Dripping in blood, the creature pulled itself out of the body, its mandibles slurping strips of flesh into its gullet.

It was a scorpion. Rob had never seen one so large. This one was at least as large as his boot. The body continued to vibrate as it crawled off of it. The mercenaries backed up, seeing two more of the creatures following its brethren out of the dead terrorist's body.

They scurried toward the mercenaries, curling their tails and opening their claws.

"No way am I getting stung by these bugs!" Steele shouted.

"Kill 'em," Rob ordered. The three of them fired a volley of controlled bursts. Their bullets punched through the arachnids, spraying black shell and yellow innards all over the cave floor. Severed tails and legs twitched as the exploded fragments settled in the dirt.

"Fuck!" Steele said. "Big-fucking-bugs!"

"Let's get out of here," Rob said. "Go out to the..." he paused, hearing a low-pitched groan coming from further within the cave. At first, he thought it was his imagination toying with him. Then it came again. It was a human voice, grunted, suppressed. In pain.

Rob aimed his light back into the interior. He panned up past a few human skeletons until his light captured a man in a white coat laying on the ground.

"It's the doc!" Rob shouted. The mercenaries ran to Bischoff's side. He was on his back, staring blankly up at the cave ceiling. Rob immediately checked for a pulse. It was faint but it was there. "Doc!" Rob lightly slapped his face. There was no reaction. Bischoff's eyes were open but he didn't move. His mouth was slack, dripping saliva and white foam. Another groan escaped his lungs. His eyes were open, though fixed on the ceiling. In addition to the leg injury, they spotted a bloodstain surrounding a hole in his shirt, which led down to a small cavity in his stomach. They wouldn't be able to find out how severe it was until they returned to the complex. Rob slung his rifle over his shoulder and knelt down by Bischoff. "Let's get him up!"

Steele had already grabbed the doctor by the arm. Together they lifted him up, each putting an arm over their shoulders. Bischoff was motionless, his legs dragging against the dirt while they moved him. Yet, he appeared to be conscious.

A wet, squishing sound drew their attention into the dark gullet of the cave. Tire-man aimed his light, seeing another terrorist corpse twitching on the ground. It too had been ripped open. The ribcage was hyper-extended as the three scorpions inside clawed their way through the meat. Claws rose from the cavity as the creatures pulled themselves out of the literal bloodbath. Their claws and tails raised high into a combative posture as the three arachnids began scurrying toward the fresh meat.

Tire-man aimed his weapon and opened fire, carefully placing three-round bursts into each of the targets. The bullets struck each scorpion along the back, exploding their bodies into gooey shards.

"Jesus, Mary…" Stroud shouted. The echo of gunfire had traveled through the mountain, escaping out through the crevice and numerous pores in the mountainside. The team converged on the side of the ledge, seeing the flashlights flickering near the mouth of the cave.

Yellowstone quickly started to climb down, followed by Muddler. Stroud and Valentine waited, ready to provide cover fire from the threat, whatever that may be.

"Rob! What's going on?!" Muddler shouted.

"Get a harness and rope from the truck," Rob shouted back. "We have the hostage! Get the rope now!"

"I got it!" Jean responded from the ledge. She hurried back to the truck and jumped inside. She dug through the supplies until she found a harness and knotted rope with a clip on the end.

Trevor limped his way to the truck, catching her on her way out. "They found him?!"

"Yes," she said.

"You don't think the specimen did all this? Could it?!"

"Not now, Trevor," she said. She ran past him with the rope. Stroud took it from her hands and clipped it to the harness. He lowered it down to Muddler, who took it and waited for their teammates to come out of the cave.

"Good Christ! There's another one!" Tire-man hollered. He aimed his MP5 at the scorpion. It scurried along the ground, the size of a school textbook, toward him. He backed up, following his team mates out of the cave. Rob and Steele had reached the sunlight, now only a hundred feet from the entrance.

Tire-man started to turn around, ready to sprint to the finish. As he spun on his feet, his light swept over the hole in the ground. It took a full second for the mercenary's brain to register the glimpse of frolicking legs and pinching claws protruding from the pore.

He turned back and squeezed the trigger. The creature launched itself across the cave. The rigid exoskeleton connected with his skull, knocking him to the ground and sending his bullets into the cave ceiling.

Gunshots and screams echoed at once. Rob let go of Bischoff and turned back, his flashlight catching brief glimpses of the enormous black shape flailing over Tire-man. This scorpion was far larger than the others. It was as large as a cow! It twisted its segmented body, tossing Tire-man around like a ragdoll. They tossed and turned, preventing Rob from getting a clean shot at the thing.

Its pincers had snapped shut on his arm, preventing him from shooting it. The claw tightened its grip, snapping the forearm. It lashed its tail, poking the stinger into Tire-man's shoulder repeatedly.

Rob stopped his advance as his ears caught the sound of scraping on the walls. He aimed his light. There was movement coming from the numerous apertures. Black arachnids snaked out one after another. In moments, the entire cave was rife with black shapes moving about.

"Ohhhh SHIT!" Steele yelled. He panned his weapon back and forth as many more creatures filled the cave.

Rob's gaze returned to the ground. For one brief moment, he saw Tire-man laying on his back, motionless as a rock. His jaw was slack, his eyes frozen in a horrific gaze, much like Bischoff. An instant later, he slipped back from view as the scorpion scurried deep into the cave with his body in tow.

Over a dozen other arachnids filled the void, preventing Rob from chasing after it.

Tire-man was gone. He had to move.

"GO! GO!" Rob yelled. He sprinted to the entrance, hearing the tapping of razor-clawed feet tapping the ground behind him. He joined Steele and dragged Bischoff from the entrance, as Yellowstone and Muddler arrived with the rope. The two of them froze, caught in a moment of shock, as they saw the group of scorpions emerging from the mouth of the cave.

"What the fuck?" Muddler mouthed. Steele worked Bischoff into the harness as Rob adjusted his rifle to full-auto.

"Take 'em out!" he ordered. He blasted his assault rifle at the front of the horde. NATO rounds struck the hard exoskeleton like hail on a rooftop. The first few cracked the shell, allowing additional rounds to breach it entirely. Chunks of black shell ripped out from the arachnid's head. Yellow blood and chunks of meat sprayed, coating the crevice with innards.

Muddler and Yellowstone joined the fray, the latter's M60 superior firing rate proving extremely useful. Shell and blood sprayed as the muscular mercenary sprayed bullets into the horde.

The scorpions scattered, with several of them circling to the left. Others went to the right, crawling up the wall to the ledge. Rob realized they were going after Bischoff.

He aimed high and fired six shots. The target's head cracked then fell apart, its brains freefalling below it. Its legs lost their grip and the creature plummeted to the ground. He fired at the next one, while Steele blasted another. Bullets hit along the target's back, cracking the shell, but not quite breaking through.

"Aim for the head," Rob said. "The shell is weakest near the eyes and mouth!"

Steele followed the example and fired. The black eyes exploded into a cloud of yellow mist, and the creature peeled off the cavern wall.

Up on the ledge, Stroud and Valentine pulled up on the rope with a combined effort. The doctor was almost at the top, hanging limp as though he was hung by the neck.

Rob reloaded and redirected his aim to the creatures closing in on the left. As he did, he glanced back to the mouth of the cave. There were more than two dozen creatures swarming out into the chasm. They were enormous, with the bigger ones being as large as golf carts. Tails curled as extended legs carried the army close to the fresh meat.

"Climb!" Rob demanded. "Muddler, go!"

"Don't have to tell me twice," Steele remarked. He slung his rifle over his shoulder and grabbed the ledges on the wall. He worked his way up as fast as he could.

"Gimme that," Rob demanded, taking the M60 from Yellowstone. "Get moving!" Both Yellowstone and Muddler hesitated, knowing Rob was going to wait behind to provide cover. There was no time to argue. They grabbed onto the rocks and climbed as fast as they could.

Rob pointed the machine gun and squeezed the trigger. The recoil was intense. It was certainly not like how it appeared in the movies, even for a conditioned soldier like Rob Cashen. His aim was all over the place with this weapon. Luckily, given the vast quantity of targets, aim wasn't really an issue. Chunks of exoskeleton popped from the black bodies as the creatures swarmed in. Dead bodies coiled and slumped to the ground, immediately covered by their brethren who crawled over them.

Rob felt something hit his shoulder. He flinched, believing one of the scorpions had worked its way along the wall behind him. A millisecond later, he realized it was the rope.

"Not gonna wait all day!" Steele yelled from the top. He kept his hands on the rope, waiting to pull Rob up.

Rob grabbed the knots and stepped up onto the protruding rock ledges in the wall. He held tight as Steele, Stroud, and Valentine worked together to pull him up. As he elevated, Rob glanced down behind him. The creatures had converged on the ground where he had stood moments earlier. Legs and pincers thrashed as though the creatures were frustrated. Backs arched as the clawed feet grabbed hold of the wall. The swarm were climbing up after him.

A spray of gunfire struck the one in the lead, sawing its face in two. Mandibles and eyes disappeared in a pool of dark yellow innards, and the creature dropped away.

Rob looked up, seeing smoke trailing from the muzzle of Jean's AK-47.

Trevor watched the team firing down from the ledge, unsure of what it was they were shooting at. There was movement in his peripheral vision. He looked up to the mountain.

He saw the black shapes emerging from those several apertures. At first, he questioned his sanity. A moment later, he realized he was not hallucinating. He thought he was looking at an army of giant ants. Then he noticed the claws. Then the stingers. They were not ants. They were worse. Scorpions.

Trevor limped to the front of the truck and climbed in. Gritting his teeth in pain, he slammed the door shut and started the engine. He put his foot to the pedal, meanwhile glancing up again at the mountainside. It was alive with scorpions. The truck gunned forward. He cut the wheel to the right, hooking the truck around until he was able to pull up next to the mercenaries.

Steele grabbed Rob by the vest and yanked him over the side of the ledge, then pointed his rifle down and sprayed all thirty rounds in his magazine into the horde below. Scorpions dropped off like dry leaves in fall, yet, the horde kept coming.

Muddler joined him in repelling the climbers. She fired short controlled bursts, keeping her aim focused on their heads. Her eyes moved to the mouth of the cave, as more scorpions continued to file out. It was obvious that they had stumbled onto their nest. The scorpions spread out, completely dominating the chasm. Others scurried back in, dragging the bodies of their brethren into the lair.

Gravel kicked up as the truck came to a stop. Trevor rolled down the window, pointed up to the mountain, and shouted, "Come on! Let's move!" The team followed his finger, seeing the swarm of arachnids descending down the mountain side. They were mere feet from the bottom, while the climbers below were nearing the ledge.

They piled into the truck, with Rob taking the front passenger seat. Yellowstone and Valentine carried Dr. Bischoff to the front and strapped him into a seat. Jean took the seat next to him and slammed a fresh magazine into her rifle as Muddler and Steele sat beside her.

Stroud climbed on up.

"GO!" he yelled. "Get us the hell out of—"

Several pairs of crab-like pincers reached up and clamped along his legs and waist. Trevor had floored the pedal, racing the truck forward. Stroud fell back, snagged in the claws of the arachnids.

"Stop!" Muddler shouted. Trevor hit the brake and Rob looked back, ready to spring into action. At least six arachnids crowded around the fallen mercenary. Stroud flailed, blasting his submachine gun wildly until the magazine emptied. The scorpions piled up on him. Several claws plunged deep into his belly and clamped shut on bone and flesh. In a combined effort, the creatures pulled apart. Stroud yelled in agony as his stomach split open. The scorpions dug in, commencing a feeding frenzy. Their claws pulled intestines and chunks of muscle tissue from the bloody gash they created. He threw his hands out wildly. Claws reached for the flailing hands and slammed shut. Bloody fingers fell free and bounced off his face. Stroud's screams turned to gurgles as the claws proceeded to tear into his lungs.

One of the scorpions took a position by his head. It extended its open claw towards his face, plunging the tip through the indentation in Stroud's cheek. He twitched violently as it closed the pincer, then savagely pulled away. It fed the cheek tissue into its mandibles, exposing Stroud's damaged cheekbone, broken teeth, and eye socket.

"Damn it," Rob cursed, lowering himself back into the seat. Muddler stood at the edge of the compartment and blasted the horde in a fit of rage. Bits of shell and yellow guts popped in the sea of black until Steele pulled her back.

Trevor floored the pedal, gunning the truck forward. Several scorpions were now scurrying the ridge like crabs on a beach. The truck bounced as it passed over them, crushing their bodies to the earth. Yellow blood pooled over the dirt as ruptured exoskeletons exposed crushed organs. Surrounding scorpions reached at the truck, grabbing whatever they could to stop the target.

Trevor spun the wheel, directing the truck toward the trail. He yelled, seeing the crowd of scorpions directly in his path. The truck hit them head-on, crushing their leader's body against the rock floor. The truck passed over it, crushing two more in the process. Tires spun against wet innards. The truck rocked a few inches but didn't go anywhere. The bodies had become jampacked under the engine. It was as if he was diving over thick icy slush.

One managed to close a grasp. Flailing its legs, it pulled itself up over the side. Another took hold on the opposite side and scurried up onto the top of the truck. Others quickly followed, while others attempted stinging the truck.

One stinger found the rear passenger tire. The air sizzled from the rubber as it deflated.

Rob aimed his rifle out of the window and discharged several rounds.

"Back it up!" he ordered. At this point, he had to treat the doctor as if he was one of his men.

Trevor put the truck in reverse and floored the pedal. The truck bounced, the spinning tires spraying scorpion guts as they fought for traction. Finally, the rubber found solid ground and launched the truck backward. He put it back into forward gear and floored the pedal again, this time steering wide of the roadkill. Several arachnids bounced off the engine as the truck sped into the dirt trail.

CHAPTER 17

The truck shook brutishly as Trevor drove it over the bumpy trail. He eased on the brakes to follow the upcoming bends in the path without toppling over.

Rob rocked side-to-side, consistently watching the side mirror. The horde was pursuing, though not as fast as the truck.

He looked up, hearing several tapping sounds from above. Battering feet echoed against the hull, followed by scraping sounds. There were scorpions on the truck. Trevor followed the curve in the road, feeling the truck starting to lean. He too could hear the tapping above him. He couldn't tell if it was one or more.

"Can you see them?" he asked Rob.

The passenger window imploded, sending shards of glass shooting across the dashboard. Rob leaned to his left, narrowly out of reach of the stinger. The rigid appendage was curved. Lime colored venom dripped from the tip as it wiggled further in. The tail wiggled like a snake, searching blindly for its target.

Rob pressed the rifle muzzle to the stinger and squeezed the trigger. The section of tail exploded into chunks of stiff shell and yellow-white organs. The tail retracted out of the window, trailing the stinger which was only attached by a few loose strands of meat.

Rob straightened himself in his seat and glanced back at Trevor.

"Does *that* answer your question?"

They both glanced at the side mirrors. They could see the scorpions hanging onto the sides, tearing into the canopy with their claws. They punctured the tarp with their claws and grabbed the rack bars, allowing them to climb over the top.

The canopy rustled then tore as pinches punched their way through the roof. The mercenaries crouched low. Yellowstone removed Bischoff from his seat and laid him to the floor to keep the scorpions from snatching him up. He aimed his M60 up at the slit directly above him.

Pincers sliced through the canopy as though it were tissue paper. The scorpion peered inside, gazing at its prey with its twelve eyes. Mandibles frolicked as though salivating.

"Eat *this*," Yellowstone said. He thrust the machine gun up into its mouth and blasted away. A barrage of bullets punched into its mouth, through its throat, and into its insides, blowing holes out its back. The scorpion fell away, only for another one to take its place.

Yellowstone aimed to fire, only to hear the tearing of tarp behind him. Pain flared in both shoulders as another pair of claws reached in and clinched down, pulling him backward. The tear in the canopy widened. The scorpion clung to the metal siding. Blood dripped from the tip of its tail where its stinger had been. Unable to paralyze its prey, it opted to hold him down for another to do the job.

Muddler and Valentine fired up at the creature peering in from the top. Its claws had coiled over its face, absorbing the brunt of the rounds. Flakes of shell rained down, followed by streams of blood.

Sensing damage to its arms, the scorpion recoiled out of sight. They could hear its feet hustling overhead, making its way down the left side where the other scorpion pulled Yellowstone back. He was now pressed against the metal siding, unable to move. The claws tightened, their razor edges drawing blood.

Steele stood up and grabbed Yellowstone by the vest. The brute yelled in pain as his teammate tried to pull him away from the arachnid's grip.

"AGH! FUCK! You have to shoot it!" he yelled.

"If I let go, it'll pull you through!" Steele said.

"Hang on to him! I can get a shot," Valentine called out. He hurried to Steele's right and pressed his submachine gun through the breach in the siding. Between the waving from the loose tarp and the frantic motion from the creature, it made it almost impossible to see its face.

Suddenly, the canopy tore open again directly above him. Valentine looked up, seeing the arachnid he had just shot. It slashed at the canopy with bleeding claws, widening the gap. He shrieked and aimed his weapon high.

The creature sprang first, tackling him to the floor.

"Shit!" Muddler yelled. She fired a shot at the beast, the round skidding over the hard shell on its back. Its body spiraled like an alligator performing a death roll, twisting Valentine's body until they both fell out the back of the compartment.

Valentine hit the ground with a heavy thud, feeling his MP5 escaping his grasp. He rolled for several feet before ending up on his stomach. He lifted his head off the dirt, slightly disoriented. He gazed back at the truck, seeing it speeding away with arachnids clinging to the side.

A hissing sound filled the air and he looked the other direction. The scorpion scuttled toward him, pincers opened wide like jaws. Valentine rolled to his back, his teeth clenched with fear. He pulled his sidearm and fired. One of the eyes exploded into strands of thin wet flesh, dangling from its face. Yet, the creature advanced, seemingly unfazed.

Nine-millimeter rounds cracked its shoulders and elbows as the creature closed the distance. Its arms lashed out, the claws cutting into Valentine. He yelled in pain, squirming and kicking desperately. The slide on his pistol locked back, the mag empty. The claws pushed his shoulders to the ground, holding him still as the tail twitched high behind the scorpion's body.

Valentine twitched and gagged, now lost in a world of panic. He could see the venom dripping from the twitching stinger.

"No! NOOOO!"

The stinger struck down, plowing through the black heart on his vest. Valentine yelled in pain. He struggled for several more seconds until the venom took hold. The strength left his body, leaving him paralyzed on the dirt. The scorpion grabbed hold of his legs and began dragging the prize back to the lair, passing the army of its brethren as they pursued the truck.

"Goddamnit! They got Val!" Jean shouted. Yellowstone was still shouting in pain as the claws held him tight against the side. Though the other arachnid was gone, it was not ready to lose its prey.

The truck rocked hard, nearly knocking Steele and Muddler to the floor. Jean staggered as well, unable to get a clean shot at the creature. She looked up, seeing the sun peering down through a widening section of canopy. There was a fourth scorpion clinging to the truck.

She aimed the rifle high.

Claws reached down and pinched the barrel. Jean shrieked as the rifle was pulled from her hands and tossed aside. The scorpion snapped its claws victoriously then angled its body to lower itself down into the compartment.

"Hit the brakes!" Rob shouted. Trevor slammed down, seeing dirt and grass spewing out from the tires.

Momentum threw both scorpions forward. Yellowstone yelled one last time as the one behind him lost its grip. It fell and rolled on the ground, its head caught under the rear tires and crushed into paste.

The remaining one up top rolled onto the truck and over the windshield. Legs scratched the glass as it propped itself up, digging a couple of feet into the engine.

Flinching legs grazed the windshield, revealing the two blade-like claws at the end of each foot. The scorpion turned and looked directly at Rob. Its tail raised high and vaulted. The barb smashed through the glass and reached in like a tentacle, stopping a few inches short of Rob's chest. The broken edges in the hole of the windshield had snagged between two segments of its tail. The arachnid pulled back, freeing its tail from the glass, and curled it back in preparation for another strike.

Rob thrust the muzzle of his rifle through the glass, pointing it at the center of the scorpion's head. A dozen rounds punched through its eyes and mouth, peeling its head outward like flower petals. The scorpion fell backward, its body crunching audibly under the truck's tires.

"My sting's worse," Rob said as he reloaded his weapon.

"You really need to work on those one-liners," Trevor quipped.

CHAPTER 18

Black tire rubber flailed in circular motions as the truck continued on the rutted trail. The flat tires in the back added to the constant juddering the truck endured and the team could feel it.

Trevor was on edge. His eyes constantly glanced between the road and the jungle. He felt the menace of every shadow. Every swaying branch made him antsy. The worst part was what he couldn't see. There could be anything beyond that wall of green. It was obvious those arachnids were not isolated to the Odessa Ridge. They had likely killed everything on this island. Now, they were the only things left on the menu.

His mind played tricks on him. At every bend of the road, his body tensed in anticipation of possibly seeing another horde of those things waiting at the other side. To add to the misery, the stress amplified the pain in his leg and jaw.

Rob noticed him squirming in his seat with a tense grimace on his face.

"Need me to take over?" Rob asked.

"No, I got it," Trevor said. He glanced back at the mirror. He couldn't see any of the scorpions behind them, then again, they had passed so many bends in the road, a clear view more than a couple of hundred feet was impossible. "You think we lost them?"

"One can only hope," Rob said. He did a check of his remaining ammo. He had three magazines remaining, one of which was already loaded into his rifle. He had three grenades and his Sig Sauer with three magazines in addition to the one already loaded. "I don't suppose those things are part of the indigenous population."

"Not exactly," Jean said. She stood up to the open panel at the front of the compartment. "We had a special hybrid, mixed with certain insect DNA with that of scorpions. We had developed an egg sack, encased in a special container. Long story short, we thought it was dead, hence it was discarded."

Muddler looked over at her, weaving a needle and thread through one of the lacerations in Yellowstone's shoulders. She tossed a piece of bloody gauze to the floor and picked up a fresh piece, while Steele worked on the other shoulder.

"How many were in that egg?" Muddler asked.

"Yow!" Yellowstone yelled.

"Hold still, you big baby," Steele said.

"Impossible in this thing," Yellowstone retorted.

"Just one," Jean answered.

"Pardon me from pointing out the obvious…but I don't think there was just ONE of those things back there," Steele said.

"I know. And I have a theory of what happened," Jean said. "I think the thing hatched, broke out of the container in search of food, and bred with a local species of scorpion."

"Then the bitch was fertile," Muddler said. "Very fertile."

"We need to get the hell off of this rock," Trevor said. He glanced over at Rob. "You mentioned that the harbor was in shambles, right?" Rob nodded. "Then we can assume they've been over there. They've probably taken over the entire island at this point. If they're multiplying as fast as they are, then we're not going to last another twenty-four hours."

"Not likely," Rob said. He stared through the busted windshield, squinting from the wind that poured in through the hole. Trevor followed another bend until finally they came to Isagana's disabled truck. Directly behind that was the juncture where the path connected with another trail leading down to the harbor. "Turn here!" Rob pointed. Trevor nodded and made the turn.

The trail sloped downward, forcing Trevor to ride the brakes as he followed the winding path.

"You sure we want to wait down there?" he asked. "Those things have already been there before…"

Rob pulled the satellite phone from his pocket.

"I'd rather wait in the open space of the beach than surrounded by jungle," Rob said.

"We could take one of the boats out," Jean said.

"No. They were both destroyed," Rob said.

"Destroyed?" Jean said. "What about the cargo ship?"

"That too. The bugs did quite the number on it," Steele said.

"On the *cargo ship*?" Jean exclaimed.

"You don't believe us? Take a look at it for yourself," Muddler said.

"No, I believe you. It's just…it's obvious their claws are sharp, but it's amazing that those things could penetrate the thick hull of such a large ship," Jean said.

"Maybe they wanted to go out for a cruise and sunbathe in the—" Trevor's joke came to an abrupt halt. Looking directly ahead, he slammed on the brakes. "Shit! Shit! Shit!"

The entire team jolted, with Yellowstone yelping as Steele inadvertently scraped his skin with the needle.

"What the hell?" the brute said.

"Up ahead," Trevor warned. Rob opened his door and leaned out for a better look. The team poked their heads out of the torn canopy and saw what Trevor was looking at.

Directly in the middle of the trail was a large mound. It was as tall as Yellowstone, and twice as wide as the one they had seen near the other Jeep trail. Rob could see the gaping pit in its center. The huge mound was like a volcano ready to explode.

"No way can this truck squeeze by that," Trevor whispered. His eyes went to the tree line, where the bones of various animals had been scattered, some still wet with innards. He did his best to control the panic that was building within him.

"I can plant explosives on it," Yellowstone said. "Just cover me."

"Idiot," Muddler said, slapping him on the arm. "Those things will pull you right in!"

"Shhh!" Rob held a hand out, warning everyone to keep calm. "Back it up slow," he said to Trevor.

"Where are we gonna go?"

"To the bridge," Rob whispered. "No choice. We're gonna have to take the trail all the way back to the facility. Let's get there in once piece, then we'll figure out what to do afterwards."

Trevor put the truck in reverse and gently eased on the accelerator. The engine revved and the tires rolled along the dirt, pushing the truck away from the mound. Rob kept his rifle pointed through the hole in the windshield, ready to open fire on any oversized critter that could emerge any minute.

Nobody moved a muscle. The mercenaries kept perfectly still, as though the scorpions could detect their movement. Jean watched through the panel with baited breath.

The truck gradually went back around the bend.

Jean tensed, hearing a tattering sound from outside. Steele joined her at the panel and looked ahead, anxiously trying to see if any scorpions were crawling out of the mound. The lair was out of sight, blocked by a wall of trees. There wasn't anything moving up ahead. Yet, they could hear the tattering.

A series of hisses filled the air. It was not coming from the front, but from the back!

They all turned around at once.

Directly behind the truck were eight or nine scorpions scurrying down the trail. Claws pulled back by their heads, ready to lunge at the soft meat. Tails coiled and twitched, while mandibles twisted below their many ghastly eyes.

"Floor it!" Steele yelled. He pointed his rifle and opened fire at the nearest scorpion. Its body shook as bullets battered its shell. It took ten bullets to crack through its back before several more cut into the loose meat inside of it. Steele sucked in a deep breath to overcome the burst of adrenaline, then took more careful aim at the next bug. Claws clipped the air as it came within ten feet of the rim. He aimed for the eyes and squeezed the trigger.

The scorpion convulsed, its arms and legs flailing wildly as its head peeled apart into chunks. It rolled on its back, legs curving over its belly while its tail twisted into ghastly positions.

Its brethren immediately attacked its corpse, snatching it with their claws and pulling it away, while others continued toward the truck.

Trevor floored the gas pedal and watched the road as best as he could to follow the winding trail. Driving any vehicle in reverse on uneven road was a hard-enough task. But a twelve-thousand-pound cargo truck?

Trevor tried to cut the wheel to follow the bend but was too late. The tires crunched another couple of scorpions before smashing into a tree. Muddler fell back, hitting Steele along the way. He grunted in surprise and stumbled toward the rim, only to be grabbed by Yellowstone.

The brute pulled him back and raised the M60, pointing it through the side of the truck. He opened fire, focusing his aim on one target at a time. He fired in five-second bursts, his bullets sawing through each target almost effortlessly.

Trevor put the truck in forward gear and hit the pedal again. The truck lurched as the tires pulled it from the rut, taking them once again down the trail as he readjusted. Once again, they came to the mound. He felt bile rising in his throat as he saw several black shapes swarming from its opening.

He looked to the side mirror, seeing several more scorpions advancing from behind.

"Shit, we're trapped!"

"Keep it together and TURN US AROUND!" Rob shouted. Trevor looked to the right. There was enough space between the trees for the engine to slip through. He cut the wheel hard and drove the truck into the jungle.

"Hang tight!" he yelled.

Leaves and branches smashed the windshield, chipping away at the glass. Remnants of bamboo, logs, and plants compressed onto the grill as the truck smashed through the terrain. Trevor bared his teeth, cutting the wheel back and forth to avoid smashing into trees or rolling into steep pits.

Damn I'll never complain about the trail again, he thought.

He kept steering to the right, blindly attempting to intersect back onto the main trail. Leaves ripped across the glass, blocking his view. The team held on to their seats, with Jean holding Dr. Bischoff to keep him from hitting his head.

"I think I see a clearing up ahead," Rob said.

"I see it too—UMF!" Trevor smacked his forehead against the wheel as the truck slumped down into a sharp incline. Tires spun, spewing dried soot into the surrounding leaves.

Rob opened the door and gazed down. The front of the truck had slumped into another big pit. This one was somewhat different. It was not a mound, rather just a crater-like hole in the earth.

"Shit, another one?!" Trevor muttered.

"Out! Everybody out!" Rob yelled.

The mercenaries piled out of the truck, carrying as many supplies as they could. They could hear scratching taking place beneath them as another swarm worked their way up from the pit.

"The trail's up this way," Rob shouted. He waved a hand to his twelve-o'clock, gesturing for the team to move. Yellowstone scooped Dr. Bischoff up and threw him over his shoulder like a duffle bag. Rob ran up to the brute and pulled an explosive from his vest. "Gonna borrow this."

"I'll help you," Muddler said.

"No! Get your ass to that trail!" Rob ordered. Muddler sucked in a breath, fighting the temptation to be defiant, then ran eastward, leading the others toward the trail.

Jean and Trevor followed behind, the latter wincing in agony as his injured leg endured the punishment of running.

"Come on!" Jean said, putting Trevor's arm over her shoulder. Trevor felt a hand grab his other arm. It was Steele, who tucked himself under Trevor's right arm and lifted up, helping to carry him up to the road.

Rob could hear the snapping of twigs and tearing of leaves in the distance. He took the explosive and stuck it under the truck, reaching as far as he could to get it as close to the gas tank as possible.

The clawing beneath drew close. As soon as the device took hold, Rob jumped back. Crab-like claws reached out from under the truck, missing Rob by inches. He backed away, watching the truck nudging upward as the horde pushed up against it. Legs and tails whipped out from the space between the pit and the truck.

The ensuing horde appeared and swarmed the truck, unaware that the fresh meat inside had vacated. A few of them spotted Rob and darted in his direction. Bullets zipped from his muzzle and punched through the soft shell along their heads, spilling eyes and mouth fragments onto the ground.

He flipped the switch on the detonator, squeezed his thumb against the discharge button, then ran as fast as he could.

The device popped into a fiery explosion. The truck's near-full tank of gas ignited. The blast shook the earth. Fire and black smoke ripped out into the trees, frying dozens of arachnids along the way. Branches rained down from above, the leaves encased in flame.

Flaming gas and oil poured into the tunnel, encasing the eight-legged occupants with fire.

On the forest floor, flaming bodies scurried all over, spreading the flames further into the jungle. One-by-one, the fire took its toll on them. Arachnids curled on the ground, the smoke carrying the horrid stench of cooked blood and organs into the air. Soon, the fire began to die down, leaving crisp fractured shells laying limp in the ashes of burnt forest.

CHAPTER 19

Muddler tucked her head down as she scraped past a hundred yards of jungle. It seemed every tree, every bush, every vine was trying to trip her up. Yellowstone was directly behind her. He was like a juggernaut, absorbing everything that hit him.

Finally, they arrived at the trail. The small clearing of jungle brought much relief. Even simply having a line of sight beyond a few feet helped eased their tension.

Muddler turned around, her momentary relief replaced by worry. Smoke ripped out from the trees, covering the sky in a thick black cloud. The hot air mixed with the stench of cooked meat, which made its way into their nostrils. Trevor coughed, trying hard not to retch.

"Rob!" Muddler yelled.

"Hey, old man!" Steele yelled into the jungle.

"Fifty is not old!" Rob's voice called back.

"Fifty-five," Steele retorted. Rob pushed through some thorn bushes and stepped onto the trail. His face was blackened with smoke. He took his glasses off and cleaned the dark stains off with a small rag.

"Did you get them all?" Yellowstone asked.

"Are you kidding?" Rob said.

"Those things are probably all over the island," Jean said.

"Why haven't we seen them until now?" Steele asked.

"If I had to venture a guess…" Jean thought for a moment, "they probably stick close to their nests during the day. Even in the jungle, they don't venture out too far until dark. Every time we saw them, it was when we stumbled close to a nest."

"There were two of those apertures in close proximity of each other," Trevor said. "They've probably tunneled all over this island."

"Then there's probably others close by," Rob said. They all looked toward the woods, hearing wet hissing sounds, followed by fluttering movements. "I'm not enthusiastic about sticking around to find out. Come on."

The team could see the pond up ahead. Droplets of sweat trickled from their foreheads as they boarded the incline and raced across the wooden structure.

Jean followed behind Yellowstone, who still carried Dr. Bischoff over his shoulder. She noticed slight movements from the doctor. At first, she thought it was from the running.

Suddenly, his body arched slightly, a dull moan vibrating from his throat.

"Hey, stop!" Jean said. They were halfway across the bridge. Yellowstone could feel the slight squirming motions from the doctor. Perhaps the paralysis was wearing off. He put Bischoff down, carefully laying him on his back. His face was still blank, his mouth slack, though his fingers were now twitching. His lips quivered and a whisper passed from his vocal cords.

"I think he's trying to say something," Trevor said.

"Dr. Bischoff, you're okay," Jean tried to sound reassuring. "This is a rescue team. They got you out of the nest."

"L—leave—" the words were barely audible. His whole jaw trembled as Bischoff fought for control. "L—ea—ve...meh."

"Doc! We're not leaving you," Jean said.

Steele looked back at the jungle behind him. Out of the green jungle came five or six black scorpions.

"Oh, great," he said. "Guys, we've got company." Rob glanced back and groaned in frustration.

"These bastards won't quit."

"We won't be able to outrun them," Jean said.

"We can't stand toe-to-toe with them either," Muddler said as she and Steele took firing positions at the edge of the bridge.

"What about the Dodge?" Trevor asked. "Can't we overturn it and see if we can get it working?"

Yellowstone shrugged his shoulders. "Beats running three miles to the facility."

"They'll swarm us before we can get that thing started...if it'll start at all!" Jean said.

"Make a decision soon, we're drawing a crowd!" Steele shouted. There were now at least ten scorpions out in the trail, and it was obvious that they were the first of many.

Rob stepped up to Yellowstone. "Take off that vest!"

"No dinner and movie first?" Yellowstone joked as he unzipped the front of his vest. He slipped it off, his enormous muscles nearly bulging right through his black undershirt as he handed it to Rob.

"You wish," Rob said. "Hold off these bastards while I set the explosives."

Jean stepped forward. "I can help!"

"Did they teach you to handle plastic explosives in the Air Force?" Rob asked.

"We had a base that housed a demolition team. I had spare time and was bored, so I took the opportunity to learn a few things," she said.

"Good enough," Rob said. He tossed her a couple of blocks of C4. They both knelt down and lifted Bischoff off the planks and carried him to the other side of the bridge. Rob set the vest down and pulled another couple of blocks of C4.

"Make it fast, because I'm on my last ammo chain," Yellowstone said. He picked up his M60 and propped it at the center of the bridge ramp. The scorpions were about a hundred feet away. Yellowstone propped the stilts and pointed the muzzle at the center of the advancing horde.

The scorpions snapped their claws, eager to tear into the fresh meat. They advanced with no sense of fear, no understanding of self-preservation beyond feeding their bellies and destroying anything that threatened their hive. Yellowstone opened fire. The target shook and reeled backward, its underside splitting open. Blood sprayed as it rolled onto its back, covering its brethren in its innards. Muddler focused her MP5 submachine gun on the right of the group. Nine-millimeter rounds struck the face of her target, punching holes through the hard casing. The scorpions writhed, confused about the invisible force that was assaulting its face. She hit it again with another burst. The scorpion lurched up, flailing its arms and tail, striking several of its brethren as it descended into a crazed, spinning motion. Several of them turned and converged on the injured member, tearing claws and stingers into its belly.

It seemed they had no problem going after their own kind for sustenance. The team continued sending volleys of bullets into the scorpions, the M60 swiftly killing each target it hit. Blood and brains sprayed, while shards of exoskeleton bounced into the trees. As they fired, they watched the horde rip at various body parts. One grabbed the tail with its claws and pulled back. The loose shell between the segments snapped. Tendons and muscle pulled apart, spraying blood into the crowd. The tail snapped free. Immediately afterwards, the scorpion holding it flailed its tail and legs against several others that clamored for it. Meanwhile, the feeding frenzy continued, with several claws pulling the misfortunate member's belly open. Heart, intestines, stomach, and other organs were exposed to the world for a mere moment before the arachnids tore into the cavity.

Rob knelt down at the side and planted a charge by one of the bridge supports. He quickly worked his way to the next one while Jean planted explosives on the opposite side.

It came back to her as though she was still in the service. She inserted the triggering mechanism and strapped the block tightly to the beam. It was the last of her two explosives.

"You think we'll need any more?" she asked.

"No, this should do it," Rob called back.

"Okay, I'll get the detonator," Jean said.

"Give me a sec, I'm almost done with this bad boy," Rob said.

Jean hustled back to the end of the pond, where Trevor waited with Dr. Bischoff. She picked up Yellowstone's vest and dug her hand into one of the pouches, finding the detonator. She activated it and made sure its frequency was aligned with the triggering devices.

She felt the hairs on the back of her neck rising as she heard bushes rustling in the jungle. Footsteps pounded the ground. She tried to turn around but was too late.

Isagana burst from the tree line, a psychotic half grin-half snarl creasing his face. He threw an arm out, wrapping it around her neck and pinning her close to his body. Jean struggled, only to stop when she felt the muzzle of a pistol pressed against her temple.

"NO!" Trevor shouted. He marched up to the terrorist leader, fists raised. Just then, another Cobra dashed out from the trees, charging the scientist. The butt of a rifle struck Trevor in the jawline, breaking his already cracked tooth. He spun and fell, spitting blood onto the dirt.

Rob stood up and grabbed for his rifle.

Isagana already had his pistol pointed. He squeezed the trigger, firing a single round. It stuck Rob in the vest just below his heart, knocking him backward.

Muddler, Steele, and Yellowstone turned their heads to the sound of the gunshot. They saw Isagana holding Jean hostage.

The bastard! He was still alive! His face was marred from an endless retreat through the jungle.

A third Cobra terrorist stepped out of the jungle, pointing his rifle down at Trevor. Isagana bent his elbow around Muddler's neck, his hand clutching the detonator.

"Thanks for doing the hard work for me," he laughed. He saw the mercenaries on the other end ready to charge. He held the device up, teasing them with it. "You make one wrong move and I'll blow that bridge right out from under you!"

"Go fuck yourself!" Steele said.

Isagana smiled then pointed a finger past them. "Pardon me from pointing out the obvious, but it looks like you've got something there."

The bugs were still approaching. The mercenaries resumed blasting away at the horde. Legs and claws convulsed as another scorpion absorbed numerous bullets through its head. Mandibles fell free, then was quickly covered by a stream of blood and brain tissue.

Rob sat up, holding a hand over his bruised chest.

"Ah-ah!" Isagana warned, this time pressing the pistol harder to Jean's temple. Rob froze, unable to move without risking the scientists or his team. The two Cobras quickly approached Dr. Bischoff and grabbed him by the arms.

Jean scowled as they forcefully lifted him off the ground. She watched Bischoff teetering on his feet as they held him up. His facial expression had changed. He was visibly in discomfort. His head bobbed as his body twitched.

A side effect from the venom wearing off?

"I see the bug experiment worked after all?" Isagana said to her. His arm tightened, nearly closing her airway. He leaned his face closer to hers. The maniac was HAPPY about this.

"They're out of control," she said.

"These ones are," Isagana said. "But not the next. You're gonna come with me off this island. Now we have proof that we can create these weapons. Our funders will give me a new facility in a new location, with more scientists!"

"You're fucking insane," Trevor groaned. "We've warned you from the get-go, though these are man-made hybrids, you'll never control them!" A kick from one of the terrorists blew his air out. Trevor rolled to his side, pressing his hands to his ribs.

Rob was back on his feet, his hand eager to go for his pistol. Behind him, his teammates were slowly backpedaling onto the bridge. Gunfire repeatedly crackled through the air. Yellowstone sprayed his M60, feeding the last of the ammo chain into the port. The finishing bullets made fast work of the scorpion they struck, which jolted ferociously as it was struck in the eyes and shoulders.

"Shit," he said. He tossed the empty machine gun down and grabbed his MP5. As he opened fire, Steele reloaded. He was down to his last magazine, as was Muddler.

Isagana and Rob locked eyes, sharing a medieval hatred for one another.

"You lost again, Cashen!" Isagana said. "Now you can join that runt that was dumb enough to tag along with you last year. Ah, I still remember the twitching of his body as I cut his throat." He closed his eyes and smiled. It took everything for Rob not to charge, but he couldn't risk encouraging the terrorist to detonate the bridge.

Isagana backed up along the trail, pulling Jean along with him. They slowly moved away from the bridge. Isagana's thumb moved over the trigger. His smile widened.

"Hey!" the guards yelled. Bischoff convulsed in their arms. His groan turned into a pained scream. Blood spat from his mouth and his body twisted and turned. The terrorists let go, letting him fall to the ground in a violent spasm.

"Pick him up!" Isagana yelled. The Cobras glanced nervously at him, them moved back in, only to jump back once again as blood sprayed from Bischoff's chest.

Jean screamed as Bischoff's back arched. Another spasm struck hard, causing his spine to snap. Blood sprayed from his chest and stomach like a fountain. Out of the spout, three black shapes emerged. Scorpion offspring, each the size of sewer rats, pulled themselves out of Bischoff's body.

The sight of fresh prey triggered their instinct to kill.

They leapt from their host in a springing motion. Isagana yelled as he saw the black legs and claws outstretched toward him. He followed the impulse to evade, diving to the left, letting go of Jean. She hit the ground and looked back. The scorpion landed in the bushes and immediately came scurrying out toward Isagana, who sprung to his feet and fired his pistol at it.

Clouds of dirt erupted as bullets struck down around the small, fast-moving target. It jumped again, landing on his waist. Isagana shrieked and fell backward, losing the detonator in the process.

Jean shot to her feet and ran to Trevor. He propped himself onto his good leg and moved as fast as he could away from the chaos.

Isagana kicked and rolled. Finally, a swipe of his pistol knocked the scorpion away. It righted itself and darted at him again, tail looped over its back.

Its brethren darted at rapid speed toward the other terrorists. Bullets sprayed wildly from their AK-47s, kicking up residue around the arachnids.

One of the Cobras screamed as a scorpion scurried up the pantleg and onto his stomach. Like a grasshopper, it jumped up over his rifle onto his neck. The stinger struck rapidly. The terrorist screamed and ran, dropping his rifle while clawing his neck.

His comrade fired at the other scorpion infant, missing as it darted left and right. Finally, his bullets found their mark, hitting the arachnid behind the head, bursting its body to pieces.

He laughed triumphantly, only to feel several piercing jolts enter his chest.

Rob looked down the iron sights of his pistol and fired again, finishing off the distracted terrorist.

The other had fallen to his knees, still screaming in pain. The scorpion pinched its claws over his hands, cutting deep into his palms. The hands retracted and the scorpion worked its way up over his face. Its twelve eyes glared directly into that of its victim. The tail vaulted over its head, driving the stinger deep into the pupil.

The terrorist gagged once more, then fell on his back. He lay motionless on the side of the trail. With the prey successfully subdued, the baby immediately noticed more prey nearby. Born with a desire to serve the hive, the small creature zipped along the ground, raising its tail and claws.

Rob pointed his pistol down at the arachnid. It moved fast and unpredictably. It zigzagged to and fro. He squeezed the trigger, missing it. Repeated shots kicked up dirt around it. The scorpion zagged right and left then finally aligned itself for a jump. It was six feet from its target. He saw the bending of its legs as it prepared to leap.

Rob fired again. The scorpion jumped, putting itself right in the bullet's path. Its body snapped in two, with its legs and tail still waving as the halves hit the ground.

"Come on!" Steele said. The team backed across the bridge, continuing to lay down suppressive fire at the incoming horde. They had to keep up the onslaught, or else the horde would quickly overwhelm the bridge. Clawed feet scraped the wood planks as the scorpions followed their prey onto the bridge.

Steele fired another burst into another arachnid then watched its faceless body slump onto the wood.

"I'm out!" he announced. He drew his pistol and squeezed off rounds.

"I'm almost out too," Muddler said.

Isagana stood up and pointed the pistol with both hands. The first two rounds missed and disappeared into the dirt. He squinted and placed his aim carefully. He squeezed the trigger, seeing the instantaneous effect of the arachnid bursting into globs of yellow blood.

He spun on his heel, ready to direct his aim at Rob.

Running feet drummed against the ground as the mercenary charged the terrorist. He was just a step or two away when the muzzle pointed at his chest. Rob threw a kick. His boot struck the pistol under the grip, launching it high into the air.

The terrorist closed his fists and lunged.

Rob swept a hand low in a clockwise motion, blocking a kick to his midsection. Isagana growled fiercely and stepped inward, throwing a punch to the face. His fist found nothing but air as Rob sidestepped. Lightning fast hands caught the arm in mid-strike, twisting the wrist and elbow. Rob twisted his hips and yanked down on the knotted arm, throwing Isagana to the ground.

Isagana landed in a summersault, settling briefly on his back before springing to his feet.

"I'm out," Muddler said. The team had now crossed the bridge. Steele reloaded his pistol as Yellowstone started firing his final magazine.

The brown wood was now covered in a sea of black moving bodies. The scorpions packed themselves into the bridge, climbing over their dead brethren. Jean ran past the brawl and grabbed the assault rifle from one of the dead terrorists. "Heads up!" She slammed a fresh mag into the rifle and tossed it to Muddler. Jean quickly grabbed the other one, reloaded it, and assisted the team in repelling the scorpions.

Isagana closed the gap and threw another punch. Rob blocked inward, his hand grasping his opponent's wrist. He crossed the arm over Isagana's chest, forcing his posture to twist. Still holding on to the wrist, Rob leaned in and grabbed Isagana by the back of the head, then pulled down, while simultaneously thrusting a kick into his knee.

His momentum was directed toward the ground. Isagana's chin hit the dirt audibly. He scrambled on all fours until he was back on his feet. Blood trickled from his mouth as he faced Rob again. Now he was furious, his scowl displaying bloodied teeth.

"I'm gonna kill you."

He charged again and threw a high kick at Rob's face. In a blur of motion, Rob snatched his leg, twisted it at the knee, and locked it up. He kicked down with all of his might, connecting his heel into Isagana's other leg. The terrorist yelled in pain as the joint bent backward and snapped with an audible crackle. He lurched backward, freeing his other leg. He miraculously managed to stay upright, teetering heavily on his good leg.

His foot bumped something on the ground. Isagana looked, realized his pistol was right underneath him. With a maniacal yell, he snatched it up and immediately raised it to aim at the mercenary.

Rob had already made his move. He reached out and grabbed Isagana by the arm, hyperextended it, and snapped it at the elbow. The terrorist convulsed in agonizing pain, the gun flinging from his hand. Rob pulled back on the broken arm, squaring up Isagana's stance.

There was a brief glance, Rob's eyes reliving the moment Isagana murdered his pupil. And now, his revenge had come at last. He rammed a fist into Isagana's throat, imploding his airway.

Isagasa hit the ground on his back, gasping for air. His face quickly lost its color while his vision blurred.

Rob stepped forward, tempted to draw his knife and finish him off. The sound of gunfire redirected his attention to the bridge. The scorpions had nearly crossed over. The explosives were still in place, ready to be detonated. But the scorpions were close to crossing. Something would be needed to hold them back, even if only for a few seconds.

He glanced back at Isagana.

"Why don't you come meet your pets?!" He grabbed Isagana by his vest and dragged him toward the bridge. Trevor met him along the way, holding the detonator in his hand.

"Want this?" he said.

"In a sec," Rob said. The team moved out of the way as he reached the foot of the bridge. Isagana glared at the horde, wide-eyed, then tried to pry Rob's hands off of him with his one arm. An elbow to the nose ended that final struggle. With a swinging motion, Rob threw the killer into the horde of black.

Hungry scorpions converged on the fresh meat. Isagana gurgled as pointed claws lanced through his ribcage. Stingers struck down everywhere, ripping holes in his flesh. Pincers closed on his arms and legs. He felt the tugging of limbs and the cracking of bone that followed before his arms came off entirely. Blood splattered the swarm, enticing them further. Intestines uncoiled all over the bridge, with several arachnids fighting over each piece of meat.

The mercenaries backed away. Rob extended his hand and accepted the device from Trevor and pressed the button.

Several loud bangs shook the jungle as the bridge went up in a cloud of flame and smoke. Fragments of wood and arachnid arched through the air, falling into the watery cavern below. Bugs thrashed in the water, some still fighting over the remaining scraps of Isagana.

Across the bridge, the rest of the swarm gathered at the ledge, watching the soft meat across the lake.

"How deep is that water?" Steele asked.

"It's deep," Jean answered, watching the bugs disappear below the surface. On the opposite side of the bridge, several arachnids crowded the edge of the lake, shrieking and fighting each other for space. Some of them dared to stick their legs into the water, only to withdraw. "It doesn't look like these things can swim well," she said.

Muddler looked back at Isagana's corpse.

"The bastards lay eggs in their prey," she muttered. "Scorpions don't do that. Do they?"

"They aren't normal scorpions," Trevor muttered, his face going pale. A mixture of exhaustion and the sight of Bischoff's ravaged body was proving too much. "Can we please get out of here?"

Rob reloaded his pistol.

"Let's get out of here before they find a way across."

CHAPTER 20

"Okay, careful! Careful!" Rob directed as Steele and Yellowstone pushed the pickup truck back onto its tires. It teetered on its side and fell back on its wheels, bouncing with a metallic crunch.

Steele immediately moved to the engine and pulled the hood. It did not want to give at first, being in such bad shape. There were many deep grooves in the hood that clearly reached down into the engine. Steele pulled up on the hood but it was stuck on something.

"Fuck!"

"Let me try," Yellowstone said.

"Be my guest," Steele retorted. Yellowstone took his place and yanked hard on the hood. There was a loud POP and the hood broke off entirely, exposing a black, leaky engine. "Well, this doesn't look good."

"You think it'll get us to the harbor?" Jean asked.

"Tire-man would've been able to fix it up well enough to do that," he said. "Not me though. I'm no mechanic." He examined the belt, alternator, spark plugs, and cylinders. "At best, it might get us back to the lab."

"I'll settle for that," Trevor said. He was seated on the ground, clutching his leg.

"We'll get you some painkillers once we're there," Jean said. Trevor nodded.

"Then we can get the hell out of here," he said. He stroked her engagement ring with his finger. "I think we put it off long enough." She smiled.

"It's about time," she said.

"Good God, it's like watching *Lifetime TV*," Steele said.

"What about when we get to the facility?" Muddler asked. "Should we head straight down to the harbor from there?"

"We know those scorpions have been to the beach before," Yellowstone said. "It's gonna be a couple of hours before pickup will arrive. I'm not sure how keen I am on waiting out in the open."

"Yeah, but we're losing daylight," Muddler said. "Do we really want to risk being here at night?"

"We've seen traces of those things all over the place, but not near the lab," Rob said.

"Maybe they're allergic to bug spray," Steele joked.

"Actually…that's it," Jean said.

"Beg your pardon?"

"Isagana's team have been spraying pesticides constantly around the facility since they've been here. They've been going overboard, spraying three times as much as they should have. The mosquito population was getting out of control after they killed our maintenance man. They weren't spraying around the harbor or construction site, and the scorpions attacked there. That's probably why the lab has remained untouched."

"I guess it makes sense. Bugs are still bugs, even if they are seven feet long," Rob said.

"Do they have any of that poison remaining?" Muddler asked.

"In the maintenance shed," Trevor asked. "Believe me, I sat next to it while getting my ass chewed by ants."

"Then we'll hole up there," Rob said, his voice decisive. "We'll fill the jungle with poison then fix up one of the Jeeps. Once pickup arrives, we'll hightail it out to the harbor, get on the plane, then get the hell out of here. Then possibly retire."

Steele chuckled. "Rob, you'll never retire. You'd get too bored."

"Maybe," Rob said. "Unfortunately, I don't know what other profession to take at this point."

"You could run a pet shop," Muddler joked. The group laughed.

Yellowstone sat in the driver's seat and turned the ignition. The engine sputtered and died.

"Come on. Come on," he repeated. He tried again and again. Finally, the engine started. The sounds were clunky, the exhaust black as ash. "Alright get aboard. If we're lucky, we can get to your lab before this thing quits on us."

CHAPTER 21

Silver moonlight broke through the canopy, casting its reflection on clouds of greyish-blue mist. The poison gas rolled through the jungle like giant ghosts, casting their deadly touch on every blade of grass, every tree, and bush in their path. The poison cannister resembled a flamethrower unit strapped to Yellowstone's back as he stepped through the jungle. He twisted a knob on the shaft, spraying another thick burst of poison into the trees. The big clouds swirled, forming a miniature hurricane. And in the eye of it was the complex, where the others were busy fortifying the research facility and gathering weapons.

Footsteps tapped the ground behind him.

Yellowstone spun on his heel and reached for his Desert Eagle.

"Whoa!" Steele said, pointing both hands up.

"You'll get your ass shot off doing that," Yellowstone said.

"That would be my luck," Steele quipped. "Survived a small army of terrorists, now on the run by big genetically engineered bugs, only to get shot by one of my own teammates."

"The only question would be whether or not it was an accident," Yellowstone added. They both cackled. The relief was short lived. Sharp hissing drew their attention back toward the trees. The horde was back there somewhere within that maze of jungle.

Those hisses were joined by sounds of clawing and ripping. The creatures were moving about, though not advancing toward the complex.

"Where the hell are they?" Steele asked. "You think they're circling the place?"

"No..." Yellowstone said. He listened to the sounds for a few moments longer. "They found where we placed the terrorists."

"Good," Steele said. "Let 'em have 'em. Maybe they'll get so full they'll go into hibernation for a month."

The hissing and ravaging intensified into what sounded like a chaotic feeding frenzy.

"I'm not staying here to find out," Yellowstone said. "This poison should drift for a while. Hopefully it'll be enough to keep them at bay."

"Do we have more?"

"A little more. We'll have to use it conservatively it we want it to last the night," Yellowstone answered. There were the sounds of fighting. Twigs and bamboo cracked as bodies tussled in the distance. The mercenaries were not keen on waiting in the jungle to figure out the outcome. "Don't know about you, but I'm going indoors."

"You can count me in," Steele said. He watched the canvas as he backpedaled toward the complex. The clouds of poison did little to ease his nerves. His imagination played havoc on his senses. The jungle was worse at nighttime. Now anything that moved appeared as though it had eight legs and crab-like claws. He turned and shuddered nervously, seeing a long, coiled malformation forming along the trunk of a tree.

He had nearly depressed the trigger on his rifle before realizing it was just a thick vine that grew on the bark.

"Fuck," he muttered.

The openness of the front lot was welcoming as the two mercenaries stepped out of the tree line. White streaks of light from the porch lamps clashed with the silvery glow from the moon, giving the lawns an otherworldly glow.

"Hey! Watch it!" It was Muddler's voice. Yellowstone glanced down at his feet. He had nearly set off a trip flare that Muddler had set up. He stepped over it and shot her a glare.

"Thanks for letting me know," he groaned.

"Hey, that's what you get for taking a thousand years to spray the forest," she said. "We were starting to think you became a midnight snack for those things."

"No, they've found their midnight snack, believe me," Steele said.

"You got trip wires all over the perimeter?" Yellowstone asked.

"Yep. Every square inch is covered. It those things come crawling in, we'll know," Muddler said.

"Lovely," Steele said. "It'll be like the microwave beeping once the burrito's been heated."

"Relax," Yellowstone said. "That poison will drift and we'll be fine. Besides, there's a reason I took so long."

"Porn magazine break?" Steele asked. Muddler rolled her eyes.

"No. I placed mines. Not everywhere, but if those things come in a swarm, there's no doubt at least one of them will trip up on one of the charges."

"How far out?" Muddler asked.

"About a hundred meters or so past the perimeter. That's assuming they're even willing to venture that close."

"We'll still have to get out of here," Steele said. He marched up to the north lot and opened the hood to one of the Jeeps. He had a set of tools placed by the tire as well as a jack. He had done some car maintenance before and after his days in the service, though he wasn't nearly as handy as Tire-man was. However, in the years they'd known each other, Tire-man had taught him a few various tricks, including swapping parts from two damaged vehicles to get one functional again. Steele got to work dismantling the engine as best he could. Bullets had punched through the grill and pierced the bearing and lever, as well as nicking the serpentine belt.

He had the hood of another Jeep open as well. That one had taken more extensive damage in the cylinder block and alternator, thanks to a few stray M60 rounds. However, the parts the other engine needed were intact.

"One of you knuckleheads give me a hand…"

****

Trevor leaned back in the lounge chair. He felt light as a feather as the morphine did its work. His leg was propped up on the coffee table, properly set and placed in a cast thanks to Rob and Jean. His leg no longer throbbed, nor did his jaw for that matter. He was lost in a bliss. It was as though there was no terror lurking beyond those trees outside. Jean sat on the couch and watched the painkillers do their work. Their hands and wrists were nearly blistered from boarding up the windows to seal off the breached balcony. Trevor's hands had ached as well, though he had already forgotten thanks to the morphine.

Rob walked up the steps after inspecting the back entrance and basement levels. He had his phone in hand and was glancing at it every few seconds, as though pestering for it to ring. He had spoken with Jayson and reported the completion of the job and the need for immediate extraction. But like most government officials from almost every country, he was asked to wait. The irritation was migraine inducing.

"Got any of that stuff left over?" Rob asked jokingly, seeing a slight grin on Trevor's face. Jean smiled.

"No military regulations to hold you back," she said.

"Give it to the bugs," Trevor said. "They'll be too stoned to chase after us." He noticed Jean's smile disappear. Suddenly, her face turned pale. Trevor sat up straight. "You okay?"

"Yeah…I'm okay," Jean's voice choked. She sounded in a crossroads of vomiting and breaking into tears. "It's just, those things that came out of Dr. Bischoff…"

Trevor nodded. In his bliss, he had already put the memory out of his mind. But now it was coming back in full force. In a way, he felt responsible, and he knew that's why Jean was so upset. Of all the gruesome experiments that had survived, it had to be those damned arachnids.

Trevor looked over at Rob. "I'm glad you fed that bastard to those things."

"Too bad they didn't take him to their lair and lay eggs in him as well," Jean grumbled. "Would've loved for him to suffer the way Bischoff did."

"It seems like these things have various feeding habits," Rob said. "Either they'll eat you on the spot or take you back to the chasm and insert eggs in you."

"Probably depends on how hungry they are," Trevor said.

"We've hardly seen a thing on this island," Rob said. "We saw a boar near the construction site. Other than that, not a thing. If what we saw is representative to the status of life on this island, then they're not only hungry, but starving."

"Then that damn poison better work," Trevor said.

Rob glanced back at the lab. The door was propped open and the artificial womb was there on the lab table. He thought of the dead hybrid inside.

"Isagana forced you to make hybrids. Those things…they didn't look like hybrids," Rob said. "They just looked like regular scorpions for the most part."

"Probably a part of the breeding process," Jean said. "Like I said, I suspect the original experiment bred with a local species to reproduce. The offspring are mainly regular scorpions affected by the CV-30."

"But the original was a hybrid? Mixed with what, may I ask?"

Both Jean and Trevor breathed a long sigh.

"Isagana went nuts on this one. I'm shocked it, of all the experiments, was the one to survive," Trevor said.

"There was DNA of fire ants placed in there. Then he had us mix in the cells of a spider wasp. They sting their host, paralyze them, then lay eggs while the host is still alive," Jean explained. "Sound familiar?"

"The ant DNA explains why they operate as a single nest," Trevor added.

"Then I imagine that bitch is far uglier than the rest of them," Rob said.

"She's the freaking mother of them all," Jean said. "An Empress."

"Where the hell is she? Dead?" Rob asked. "They seem to have no qualms about eating each other. Explains why we've only seen slight traces of them before."

"I hope so," Jean said.

The phone rang with an obnoxious techno beep.

"Finally," Rob said. He pressed the receiver button and held the phone to his ear. "This is Cashen."

"Jayson speaking. Here's the situation. We're watching via satellite right now. There are U.S. Air Force jets patrolling the skies near Hollow Mauna. We can't get you at the moment until the patrols are clear."

"What the hell are you talking about?!" Rob growled. His hand tightened into a fist, turning the knuckles bone-white. "This place is crawling, you hear me? Your infamous colonel has been tampering with biological engineering. I've lost three men already because of the outbreak!"

"I understand, Mr. Cashen, but as I have stated before, it is my job to keep this situation quiet. We can't keep this on the down-low if we fly in while American patrols are in the area."

"All I'm hearing are excuses," Rob said. "If you're trying to bury us as a loose end, believe me you will lose, and I'll spread the news all over the place that your government had created the next terrorist organization that bombed Japan and China."

The line was silent for a moment.

"Mr. Cashen, we are monitoring the jets and carriers. As it stands, we might be able to launch at 0430. Add a couple hours of flight time, and we should arrive at dawn if all looks well."

Rob's fist tightened.

"Assuming we last until dawn," he said.

"We will notify you when the flight leaves the carrier," Jayson said. "Just hang tight. We'll be there at sunup." The line went dead.

The other three mercenaries hustled into the first-floor lobby, having heard the long-awaited ringtone.

"What's the word, boss?" Muddler asked.

"We're gonna have to wait here tonight," Rob said.

"You've got to be shitting me!" Steele snapped. He turned and kicked a trash can, sending it bouncing across the lobby, spilling its contents.

"Steele, quit whining like a little girl," Rob said. "Yellowstone. How much pesticide do we have left?"

"Depends on how you want me to utilize it," Yellowstone said. "The jungle's pretty saturated right now for over a hundred meters. To make a similar cloud of the same proportion, then we have enough for one more dousing. Or I could lightly spray the perimeter and drag it on out for the rest of the night."

"You have the mines set up?"

"Correct," he answered. "And Muddler has trip flares in place in case any do get through."

"Good work. We'll wait for now," Rob said. "Steele, how's that Jeep looking?"

"Still leaking oil," Steele said. "Can't figure out exactly where it's spilling from. But we have a fresh cannister handy and it should be enough for us to get to the beach."

"Good," Rob said. "Okay, I want somebody on watch at all times. It's important we all get some rest. Each of us will do three hours."

"I'll go first," Muddler said, raising a hand.

"Okay. At 0100 hours, get me. I'll probably be a light sleeper tonight anyway. Steele, you'll be next, then Yellowstone."

"Hey! How come he gets the short shift!" Steele said.

"Because I'm sexier than you," Yellowstone retorted.

"Yeah…somehow I don't think that idea fared into his reasoning," Muddler laughed.

"Hell no. By the way, Steele, before you get some shut-eye, clean up that mess you made," Rob said, pointing down at the trash can. Steele shrugged his shoulders.

"My bad."

CHAPTER 22

The night had been surprisingly quiet. It was Rob's turn to take watch. The three-hour snooze he had taken during Muddler's tour had been more than enough. He was always a light sleeper, though in this case, he was growing restless for the inevitable journey to the harbor.

Yellowstone's earthshattering snores didn't help. The brute sounded like a giant cave troll as he slumped on the couch in the second floor lobby. Rob pressed his forehead to a wall.

Make it stop.

He had slept through artillery fire, endless rifle volleys, in the heat, cold, and none of it fazed him. Yet, Yellowstone's snoring was enough to drive him to madness.

Finally, one snore erupted into a crackling grunt. He could hear Yellowstone clear his throat and roll over.

Rob stood at the front of the lobby, embracing the new silence, however long that may last. He watched the outside through the wood planks nailed over the windows. As usual, there wasn't much to see. They had switched off the porch lights in hopes that it wouldn't attract the arachnids. In addition, a cloud had passed over the moon, blocking its silvery reflection. As it was, Rob was looking at a black abyss.

He heard footsteps coming down the stairway. He turned and saw Jean. She wiped a damp cloth over her eyes and entered the large room.

"Can't sleep?" Rob asked.

"Had the giant stopped his racket five minutes ago there'd have been hope," she said.

"I was afraid he'd bring the entire swarm on us," Rob joked. Another stunted snore echoed from above, causing both of them to glance back.

"There's still that chance," Jean said. Rob glanced at the satellite phone. He was eager to hear the news that Jayson's team was on their way.

"You should probably try and get some more rest," he said to Jean.

"How can anyone sleep?" she responded. She gazed out the window, but saw nothing but the cracks from bullet holes creasing over her reflection. She could hear the trees swaying in the wind outside. Every clash of branches made her antsy. It was hard not to let the imagination run wild. "The poison seems to have kept them back." The statement was to calm herself more than Rob. It didn't do much to ease the anxiety.

"Maybe they got enough to eat from the dead terrorists," Rob said.

"Scorpions that large would need to eat their own weight every three or four days," Jean said. Admitting that fact doubled the sick feeling in her stomach. "Even the whole squad of Red Cobras would only satisfy a fraction of the horde. And even if all of them had bellies full to the brim, they'd still be in search of live hosts for reproduction."

"Destroying them is near impossible. Can't kill them by bombing. They've tunneled all over the island. Even if they got caved in, they'd just dig themselves out. Are they able to get off this island?" Rob asked.

"I suspect they can swim short distances to catch food, but as far as traveling? No, they're stuck on this island. They will starve to death once we're gone, as long as nobody comes back to this place."

"Fine with me," Rob said. He leaned in close to the window again, still unable to see past the porch. He reminded himself that Muddler had trip flares all over the perimeter.

With Yellowstone's snoring subsided, Rob found himself getting drowsy in the silence.

"Is there a coffee machine in here somewhere?" he asked.

"Yeah, in the hall over that way," Jean said, pointing to the corridor on the left. "Go ahead, I'll hold down the fort."

"Appreciate it," he said. He stepped away and found the kitchen and immediately started scooping the grounds.

Jean watched the window for a few more seconds then felt the need to move. She started pacing along the window then stepped along the north end of the room. The mercenaries had stacked weapons and ammo collected from the Red Cobras. There was enough nine-millimeter ammo to replenish their MP5s. Unfortunately, the H&Ks took a different caliber than the AKs, resulting in the team having to use the dead enemy's weapons. Jean didn't care for the AK models. They weren't the most accurate of weapons, in fact, they were most well known for their ability to spray bullets, as well as dependability in rough terrain. It was certainly better than being without something to fight with.

She picked up a rifle and examined it. It was well cleaned, to her slight surprise. After loading a fresh magazine into it, she found a spare MP5 submachine gun. She loaded that as well then found herself a pistol and holster. It was a CZ-75, a Czech firearm with a magazine capacity of eighteen rounds. She strapped the holster to her thigh and placed the weapon inside of it.

A large boom vibrated from outside. Jean felt the earth tremble beneath her feet. Rob ran out from the kitchen back, the grogginess completely gone, replaced by a grand alertness. They both arrived at the window, and at once, they saw the orange glow behind the wall of trees.

The mercenaries gathered upstairs at the atrium.

"What's going on?! Was that a mine?" Steele called down.

"What do you think?" Rob said.

"Probably this guy's fault right here," Muddler said, nudging Yellowstone with her elbow. "Practically rang the dinner bell with his snoring!"

"I wasn't snoring," Yellowstone rebuked.

"Okay...first: Yes you were! Second, get your asses down here!" Rob demanded. The mercenaries hustled down the stairway and gathered near the front entrance.

"Any sign of them?" Muddler asked.

"Not that I can see but I think it's safe to assume they know we're here," Rob said. He switched on the porch lights and stepped outside. He advanced a dozen feet. The full moon shined down again, casting its glow over the towering mountain of smoke.

He could hear movement within those trees. Scurrying legs carried the arachnids in numerous different directions. There were shrieks and hisses, as the swarm had likely disbanded from the unexpected explosion.

There was movement heard from the opposite side of the perimeter as well. Rob listened. The bugs seemed to be moving in circles rather than swarming the complex directly.

"It's the poison," Jean said, reading his mind. "Their senses are probably out of whack at the moment. They might have even lost a few in the cloud. They're probably searching for a path that isn't soaked in the pesticide."

"They'll get courageous soon enough," Rob said. "Get that canister, big guy and start spraying!"

Yellowstone strapped the harness on and checked the shaft. He marched to the tree line, being careful not to trigger the trip flares.

"How much, Boss?"

"All of it," Rob said. "We gotta repel them back." Yellowstone aimed the nozzle and released the blue gas into the trees. It swirled and broke apart as it traveled back through the canvas. Yellowstone worked his way along the perimeter, swaying the nozzle left and right. The cloud grew into segmented bodies, almost appearing like a curling millipede of poison gas.

Steele hopped into the repaired Jeep and started the engine. He brought it close to the porch and pointed the engine toward the east trail.

"When it's time to leave, we're gonna have to go quick," he said.

"Good thinking," Rob said. Yellowstone continued spreading the cloud.

Wet sounds of squirming and twisting filled the jungle. Bugs hissed as the dense cloud made contact. Feet rustled the ground as the unseen horde turned back.

"Keep it going," Rob said, listening to the movement.

"Nah, I thought I'd stop here and fire up the grill," Yellowstone retorted.

The group waited silently as the brute completed the circle.

"Oddly enough, I could go for some smoked sausage and chili dogs," Steele said.

"It'd be a burger for me," Rob added.

"Just don't let Yellowstone cook it. It'll come out charred, as always," Muddler said.

"Best way to have it," the brute called back.

"You guys are insane," Jean said. A smile managed to break through. Yellowstone released one last spray of poison. The nozzle spat droplets as the last of the supply was expelled from the tank.

"Not insane enough to stay out here," Rob said. "Everyone back inside."

The group filed in through the front entrance. Trevor was watching through the window as they came in. Rob shut the door and bolted the lock.

"You think that'll work?" Trevor asked.

"It's held them off until now," Rob said. "We just need it to last until daybreak."

"Three...four hours then," Trevor said. They watched the window. There was no point in turning off the outside lights this time. It seemed the poison had done the trick.

"You all might as well try and get a little more rest in the meantime," Rob suggested. "You'll want to be sharp when we get out of here."

CHAPTER 23

There wasn't any sleep to be had. The distant shrieks invaded the eardrums of every person in the facility. It might as well have been deliberate psychological warfare.

Rob was the only one who appreciated the sounds to an extent. They at least reminded him that the enemy was out there. It kept him on his guard. The cloud still drifted like a fog over a lake. He wondered how many of the bugs had been killed by overexposure to it.

Steele was up on the second floor, watching the west window overlooking the back of the compound. The rest of the team waited in the main lobby, each wide awake and ready to leave at a moment's notice.

Trevor rocked in his chair, the anxiety causing the pain in his leg to return prematurely. Jean stepped out from the infirmary and gave him a small dose of morphine. He winced from the needle, then settled back, relaxed once more.

Yellowstone leaned back and clutched his knee.

"Oh, ow! I think I hurt my knee!" he joked.

"Nice try," Jean said. She tossed the needle into a hazmat bin. When she returned to the lobby, she noticed Trevor gazing at the pile of guns. He leaned on his crutch, almost appearing more nervous of the weapons than he was of the creatures outside. He leaned down and picked up a pistol.

"What are you doing?" Jean asked. He almost jumped, as though caught doing something he shouldn't have been.

"I uh," he cleared his throat, "I figured I might as well learn how to use one of these."

"Really?" she chuckled. "I thought you were a big gun-control guy from Los Angeles."

"Not anymore!" he said, nudging an elbow toward the window and the world of scorpions that lurked beyond their line of sight. Jean smiled and took the pistol from his hand. She showed him the magazine ejector, then pressed her thumb on the button. The mag slid out, fully stacked with bullets.

"Put it in like this, pull the slide back hard like this..." She demonstrated by pinching the slide and pulling it back hard. She let it go, chambering a round. "Grip it with both hands like this. Keep your thumbs away from the slide. When you shoot and that thing comes back, it'll rip your thumb to shreds." She turned the gun, displaying the safety lever. She moved it up, revealing the red dot. "This means it's ready to fire. At this point, simply point and shoot. You're not used to the recoil, so just hold on tight."

"Gotcha," Trevor said. He placed a holster on his belt then took the weapon back. Unfortunately, it was the best crash-course he would get in this scenario. They couldn't even risk going outside for a few practice shots.

Rob looked away from the window. There was nothing out there so far. He stared down at his satellite phone again.

His eyes moved to the ground. He felt something. A slight vibration under his feet. He froze, trying to concentrate on whether or not his imagination was toying with him. If a mine had detonated, they would've heard it. He looked out the window again. There were no signs of fire. He glanced up to the atrium. Steele was watching the back window and didn't appear alarmed.

Rob stood silent again. The vibration seemed to have stopped. Maybe it was his imagination after all.

The phone rang in its high-pitched techno tone. Rob nearly jumped, both out of surprise and an eagerness to answer it.

"This is Cashen."

"Good news, Mr. Cashen," Jayson said. "We have departed the carrier and are en-route."

"Estimated time of arrival?"

"Ninety minutes," Jayson answered.

"Excellent. We'll be there," Rob said. He hung up the phone. At least something was going right. He turned to face the team, expecting to see several relieved expressions on their faces. Instead, he saw confusion.

Yellowstone was standing up and looking in every direction.

"What was that?" Muddler said. She stood up as well. Rob felt it again, that strange shaking beneath his feet. It was much more intense this time.

"I didn't hear any mines go off," Trevor said.

"Nothing back here," Steele said.

The shaking intensified. Rob glanced to Muddler's water bottle, seeing the contents swishing inside. Stray ammo cartridges rolled along the floor. A glass shattered somewhere in the hallway. Now everybody was on their feet.

Trevor limped to the window. "What the hell's—" He teetered back, barely able to keep his balance.

Now it was as if the earth was shifting below them.

"Earthquake!" Jean announced.

There was a grinding sound beneath the floor. Earth and rock crunched deep within as though caught in a blender.

"I don't think so," Rob said.

Something struck directly beneath his feet, knocking him backward. The mercenaries spread out. The floor peeled out from the center of the room. Cement and dirt erupted into the air and mixed into a grey cloud.

Black pincers rose high from the pit. They were huge, as large as a man. Gargantuan arms followed them up, then bent at the elbows, digging the jagged points of the claws into the ground. Jointed legs sprawled up over the edges. They were thirteen feet in length at least. Next came the gigantic segmented body attached to all of them. The shell was black with bright red lines running along the head and back like veins.

"Fucking SHIT!" Steele yelled out. The creature hadn't even pulled its lower half free from the pit and yet, what was exposed was at least ten feet in length. She was the mother of all scorpions. An Empress.

Jean backed away, her heart pounding harder and harder. She was staring at her own creation. The Empress was a true combination of insect and arachnid DNA. She had three segments of her body, like an insect, allowing her to turn her head. Her head was angular like that of a wasp, containing two huge eyes that stared infinitely. Giant pincer jaws clamped together from its mouth. Underneath those bony pincers were small curling mandibles. They extended out as the creature bellowed at the smaller biped creatures below.

"Get out! Move!" Rob yelled.

Jean and Muddler tried to run along the wall to get to the door. Like an enormous tentacle from a kraken, the Empress' tail whipped into the air. Its curved stinger slashed the ceiling, slicing a groove in the tile. The tail vaulted, landing in the wall just inches ahead of Jean.

Muddler grabbed her by the jacket and pulled her back. The tail lashed back, yanking the stinger from the wall. The stinger struck the window, sending shards of glass and wood planks exploding onto the front lawn. The tail whipped to and fro, striking Trevor in the chest and knocking him to the floor

"Up the steps!" Steele shouted. He pointed an AKM assault rifle and pointed it down at the creature's face. Two enormous glassy eye-sacks glowed a hellish orange as they stared back at him. Almost five-feet wide, they stretched out from the center of its face, nearly appearing like a giant orange visor. Steele's ears rang as he fired off several rounds. The Empress didn't even flinch. The bullets crunched against her thick exoskeleton and ricocheted to the floor. He might as well have been throwing stones at her.

Its legs stretched and scratched razor claws into the flooring. The Empress pulled itself clear of the gaping hole in the floor. Muddler pushed Jean up the stairway. Despite her desire to help Trevor, Jean had no way of reaching him without getting scooped up by the giant.

Trevor stood up, only to duck again. The tail lashed over him then corrected into a coiled position over the scorpion's body. He gasped as he watched the jagged tip of the tail. The stinger's tip was surprisingly thin, though hard as steel. It was probably no thicker than the muzzle of his pistol.

Rob fired several shots into its side. The beast turned and fixed its eyes on him.

"Oh, shit..." he muttered. He turned and dove into the hallway. The beast lunged after him. Huge claws struck the wall and ripped outward, effortlessly tearing the plaster and studs to pieces. Rob moved further into the hall, seeing the entrance quickly widening. He emptied his magazine into its face, the confined gunshots causing his ears to ring. The beast wasn't fazed in the slightest. Even its eyes seemed to have a thick protective casing around them.

As Rob ejected his empty magazine, more gunshots filled the room. The creature backed away from the hall and turned to face its new challenger.

"Come on, queen bitch! Come get some!" Yellowstone yelled.

"No!" Rob yelled out. "Get out of here!"

Yellowstone didn't listen. He yanked a grenade from his vest and threw it at the leviathan. It bounced off the Empress' face and exploded halfway to the floor. The concussion drove the creature back a few steps.

Trevor saw the back leg moving toward him. He scurried on all fours. The floor where he laid moments ago splintered as the legs crashed down. Its exoskeleton was hardly scratched. Yellowstone's heart quickened. The thing survived a grenade blast at near point-blank range.

"Not fair..." he muttered in shock. The jaws opened wide and a triumphant screech surged through the air. It was like a supersonic surge had struck the facility. Everyone cupped their ears and winced in pain. Rob staggered back into the hall, feeling as though he'd been hit by an invisible wall.

Trevor yelped as he cupped his ears. His eyes had been squeezed shut until the deafening roar subsided. Pounding footsteps prompted those eyes to open. The creature's razor feet were closing in fast. It was sidestepping, blindly on the verge of crushing him. He pushed up onto his feet and ran as fast as he could for the door. He yanked the bolt free and spilled out onto the porch. He continued crawling, relieved to be out in the open. Yet, he felt helpless at the same time.

The Empress lunged, its shell deflecting Yellowstone's spray of bullets. He pivoted on his feet to make a mad dash for the back door. He burst between the double doors, leaving them to swing back on their own. He bounced off the back wall and turned left, about to dash down the hallway.

The doors exploded inward into fragments. Like giant shrapnel, they filled the corridor, many of them striking the mercenary in the head, shoulders, and back. Giant claws entered the corridor, splintering the corners of the doorframe. Their speed was rapid, reaching faster than Yellowstone could run. It was like a bird snapping up a grasshopper.

Razor claws tightened around his waist, drawing a crazed scream. Yellowstone arched and twisted, slamming his empty rifle against the rock-hard appendage. The Empress backed up into the lobby and raised its prize high in the air. The claws tightened. Yellowstone's yell turned to a high-pitched shriek as his spine snapped like a toothpick. Blood oozed from his waist and trickled onto the floor.

The other claw clamped down across his chest. The pincer tightened, snapping both arms below the shoulders and crunching the breast plate and upper spine. A slow, pained gurgle rolled from Yellowstone's throat as both arms pulled away from each other.

His body came in half like warm butter. Intestines uncoiled and spilled onto the floor along with stomach contents and kidneys. The Empress raised the dead mercenary high again, victorious, then fed the halves into its giant jaws, starting with the legs.

Muddler's face tightened as the creature fed on her teammate. "You...BITCH!" She pointed her rifle and fired. The Empress fed on Yellowstone's other half, unfazed by the attack.

Trevor rested for a moment. The pain in his leg was returning despite the morphine. He looked back in search of a way to get the others out.

A red flash of light streaked high into the sky like a shooting star. One of Muddler's trip flares had been triggered. He immediately remembered those had been set along the perimeter.

Like a black flood, the scorpions stormed the complex from the north. Tails arched high, ready to perform their deadly purpose. Claws snapped and mandibles twitched. Black shells reflected the moonlight like glass.

"Shit! Shit! SHIT!" Trevor panicked.

That shriek, it wasn't a cry. It was a call. And these scorpions had answered the call of their Empress.

Some moved sluggishly. Others collapsed within a few feet of the tree line. The poison had weeded through many of the weak, leaving the strong to persevere. They climbed over their dead brethren and invaded the lot.

Flares streaked across the sky as more invaded the lot. Their flickering red flames cast a hellish glow over the research facility.

Steele glanced back, seeing the fiery strobes flashing through the back window. He moved across the room and pressed his eyes to the glass.

"Oh, you've got to be kidding me!"

Jean turned and saw the window. The scorpions were all over the place, moving between the tents and up the walls.

Bulging eyes and flailing mandibles emerged from down below as one of the arachnids climbed. It appeared to stare at them for a moment before assaulting the glass with its pincers. Cracks traveled along the five-foot panel.

Steele and Jean backed away, bumping into Muddler, who scuttled back as the Empress assaulted the railing with her claws. The window came apart into jagged fragments.

"Fuck it," Steele said. He fired his rifle. Chunks of shell flew from the creature's face and spilled down into the glass along with heaps of blood. The scorpion fell backward, only for several others to take its place.

Behind him, the railing exploded. Pincers clamped down on the edge as the creature started heaving herself up over the ledge.

"This way!" Jean shouted. They ran up and around entering the hallway which led to the living quarters.

The drones swarmed into the lobby. In minutes, the area was covered by arachnids. Razor-sharp claws marked the floor as they scampered into the hall.

Trevor stood up. More trip flares soared into the air, lighting the front lawn in red. He glanced left, then right, then back. The scorpions were everywhere! He stood, frozen by fear as they advanced from all sides.

He started to hyperventilate. There was nowhere to go. Snapping claws reached forward as tails swung high like enormous worms escaping from oversaturated ground.

He forced himself to focus. The Jeep was just a few feet ahead of him. He yelped in misery as he reached the door in a single bound and dove into the driver's seat.

The keys were still in the ignition. He started the engine and felt the reverberation as it roared to life.

"Oh, thank God—" The side window shattered, spilling glass onto his lap. "FUCK!" he yelled. He leaned to the right as the scorpion tore its clampers into the door. The Jeep rocked as another attacked from the passenger side. More glass burst, the shards flying inward, nicking him in the arm and cheek.

As Trevor ducked, his elbow pressed against his pistol, reminding him of its presence.

If there was any time to man up and use it, it was now.

He yanked it from the holster and straightened himself in the seat. He twisted to the left and pressed the muzzle right at the scorpion's face.

"Die, you motherfucker! Die!" he screamed. His ears rang as he discharged the weapon rapidly. The scorpion scurried back, its face bleeding. It rolled in agony, its brain having been nicked by one of the rounds. Immediately, the scorpions around it sprang into action, ripping off legs, then plunging their pincers into the belly.

Trevor pointed the pistol to the other side and fired at the other scorpion. Blood squirted from its mouth. The creature backed off, brushing its claws over its face, as though trying to defend itself against an invisible attacker. Trevor leaned and pointed the pistol through the window, squeezing the trigger repeatedly. Two rounds fired off before the slide locked back. Trevor didn't realize this until he heard at least six empty clicks. But those rounds had hit their mark, driving the target into a frenzy. Several others converged on it, enticed by the smell of blood.

The Jeep shuddered. Trevor looked ahead. Another scorpion propped its front legs on the engine. Its arms raised high, ready to drive the pointed tips of its chela through the engine.

Trevor floored the gas pedal. Dirt sprayed from the tires as they gained traction. The Jeep shot forward, driving the scorpion on its back. Wheels crunched down on its shell as he passed over it, leaving a twisted writhing body behind.

The Jeep bounced as the engine slammed into another scorpion, smashing its head down between its shoulders. Trevor stopped and backed the Jeep up, making distance between the horde gathering ahead of it. He cut the wheel hard to the right and gunned the accelerator. He raced a wave of scorpions then spun the wheel left as he reached the perimeter. He circled the compound, swerving back and forth to avoid crashing as he watched the facility for any sign of his friends.

Rob could see that the Empress had moved forward, its attention momentarily off of him. The opportunity was now. He ran from the kitchen hall into the lobby, immediately taking a right turn to make his way to the door.

"Whoa!" He dug his heels into the floor and stopped. Several scorpions climbed their way through the busted window. They locked their eyes on him and advanced with arms outstretched. Rob fired several quick bursts of gunfire. Heads exploded into hollow husks, their brain contents spilling onto the tile. Others were quickly entering the room. Getting outside would be impossible.

Rob backed up. In the corner of his eye, he noticed the Empress beginning to rotate. Fresh blood stained her pincers, while a few entrails dangled loose from her jaws. Her feet lashed the floor, kicking up office chairs and loose flooring. Among the debris was the black supply bag stocked with ammo...and explosives.

It was only four yards away from him, but it was four yards toward the monster. It was now or never. Rob made the run, closing the bag in three strides. He snatched up the straps, turned, and dove into a summersault. The pincers came down, snapping shut inches behind him. He rolled to his feet and raced back into the hallway. The Empress lunged again. Her claws struck the wall and quickly began digging away.

Her drones swarmed the interior, filling the lobby and the back hall. Others moved up the steps, joining the pursuit of the other soft meat that occupied this artificial habitat.

Rob moved back to the end of the hallway. Already, scorpions were spilling into the corridor. He pointed his rifle, killing one. It slumped on its belly, head and shoulders spilling yellow-colored innards onto the tile. Another climbed over it, claws reached out ahead of its face. Rob fired again. Shell and blood exploded from the claws, halting the arachnid's advance. Rob continued the assault. More bullets struck the claws, busting them into fragments, clearing the path to the head. Eyes burst and shell shattered as the remainder of the magazine's payload entered its body.

More scorpions were already gathering behind the two dead ones. Rob glanced around, seeing only a few enclosed rooms with no exit. He was trapped in this hall with only two more full magazines left.

"This isn't good," he said to himself.

Jean took a right at the end of the hall where the juncture led to the front suite overlooking the front lawn. The balcony had been destroyed during the firefight. Jean looked through the doorway. Through the collapsed wall on the opposite side, she saw the front lawn and the horde that filled the lot.

"Oh, my god. We'll never get out through here," she said.

"Can't sit and wait!" Steele yelled. He was still at the corner, firing back into the hallway. The scorpions scampered up along the walls and ceiling, completely filling the corridor. With nowhere else to go, Jean entered the suite. Muddler and Steele followed, slamming the door shut and locking it.

The door immediately shook as armored bodies crashed against it.

"That's not gonna last long," Muddler said. Jean approached the ledge of the room where the balcony had been. Already, the claws of a scorpion emerged, pulling the creature up over the ledge. Jean and Muddler opened fire the moment its head emerged. Its corpse fell away, spurring the others into a frenzy below.

Headlights moved in the distance. Jean watched closely, realizing it was the Jeep. She immediately raised her hands, while Steele ignited a flashlight and waved it.

"HEY! OVER HERE!"

Trevor saw the light first. Then his fiancée. He turned the wheel, bumping into another arachnid as he tried to get close. He only traveled a few yards before being forced to turn away.

There were too many scorpions gathered below the ledge. He would be swarmed in seconds if he even got close. He turned and circled, dodging arachnids and other obstacles as he tried to muster a plan.

"Damn it! There are too many of them!" Muddler fired another volley downward, killing another arachnid. Yet, more were climbing up, while more continued to fill the yard.

The sound of wood splintering turned their attention behind them. Pointed claws punched through the door and sliced down like a sawblade. The door broke apart piece-by-piece. Already they could see the invaders through the breaches, waiting to charge the fresh meat.

Steele drew in a deep breath and shook his head.

"We're fucked."

The Empress continued carving a hole into the wall, widening the tunnel while her drones continued to crowd the entrance. Rob fired the remainder of his magazine into another scorpion. Immediately, its dead body was being trampled by its fellow creatures. Rob plucked a grenade from his vest and tossed it into the group.

He dove into the nearest room on the right and slammed the door shut. The confined blast was deafening, as were the shrieks that followed. Blood and shell sprayed the walls of the hallway, some of which leaked under the door behind him.

Rob stood up and locked the door. Behind it, the creatures had filled the hall entirely and were now clawing at it. It would be seconds before they breached. Rob had to think fast. He looked at the room. It was a utility area. The wall opposite the door would lead outside. As luck would have it, there was no door or window.

The door began to splinter.

Rob pulled a block of C4 from the bag and placed it against the far wall.

Either this works or it doesn't, he thought. At this point, if his idea 'backfired' and the explosion killed him, it would still be preferable to being eaten alive or impregnated by the scorpions.

The door began to peel apart. Snapping claws reached into the room.

Rob set a five-second timer and dashed back across the room. He dove behind the work bench and pressed his palms to his ears.

The charge detonated, blasting a hole through the side of the wall. Rob peeked from the desk. The explosion had been directed outward, sending chunks of debris out into the patio.

The door came apart entirely.

Rob dashed for the breach, dropping a grenade on the floor behind him. It rolled toward the pursuing horde and detonated, sending a gruesome aerosol of guts into the ceiling.

Rob made it out a few meters when he saw the crowd gathering on his left. Up above the pile of scorpions were the muzzle flashes from his teammates.

Bright lights consumed him.

"HEY!" Trevor called out. He sped the Jeep close by, smashing another scorpion. "Get in!"

Rob pointed his rifle and placed several shots through an advancing arachnid. He dove into the passenger seat and slammed the door shut as Trevor floored the accelerator.

"Get us close!" he said to Trevor. He opened his bag again and pulled another explosive. He set a five second timer and waited until Trevor completed his circle to activate it.

Rob leaned out the window and threw the brick like a grenade. "GUN IT!"

Trevor sped them away, drawing the attention of the horde. The charge detonated, blowing several scorpions into bloody fragments that traveled across the lawn. Fire surged along the grass and wall, driving several of the scorpions away.

Steele and Muddler returned to the ledge after taking cover. A few scorpions quickly returned to the wall while others retreated from the heat. Both mercenaries fired down at them, emptying their weapons.

The back door broke apart entirely. Jean fired back, dropping the first one that crawled through. Steele threw another grenade, bouncing it into the hallway where it detonated. The building shook as dust and debris spewed into the room.

They heard the beeping of a car horn down below.

The Jeep circled, weaving around several bugs before pulling up along the building. Rob immediately leaned out and fired at several scorpions that approached

"Come on!" Trevor screamed.

Steele pushed Jean. "GO!" She jumped down without hesitation and landed on the top.

He could hear the horde swarming the room behind him. He and Muddler stepped to the ledge. Steele jumped first, landing on the Jeep as Jean slid herself over the side. Muddler jumped immediately afterward.

Intense pain surged through her shoulders. Her fall came to a sudden stop. As though hanging by a sting, she swung back and hit the wall. She glanced up, seeing the scorpion that had snatched her in its claws. The pain intensified as it pulled up, scraping her back against the edge of the balcony.

"NO!" she screamed. She kicked her legs and twisted her body, unable to free herself from its grasp.

"Muddler!" Jean shouted, watching the mercenary's feet slip away from view.

Muddler hit the floor and immediately saw a world of black swarming over her. The scorpions wasted no time. Her body jolted with each sting. Eyes wide, Muddler grunted in pain as each one hit their mark. Blood and froth spilled from her mouth as the overdose of venom surged through her veins.

The creatures continued stinging, as though performing a satanic ritual. Others, intensely craving sustenance, immediately drove their claws into her flesh.

Paralyzed by their venom, Muddler laid helpless on the ground as the swarm dismembered her body. Pincers sliced into her arms and legs, snapping the bones and pulling them free from her torso. Other claws ripped into her midsection, slicing into her stomach and digestive tract.

"Goddamnit!" Rob yelled in anger. He could see blood spilling over the edge. Steele and Jean both sprayed bullets all around as scorpions crowded toward the Jeep. "She's gone. Get in!" he yelled.

As he spoke, the side of the building exploded out, sending chunks of brick spilling onto the yard. The Empress shrieked again, her tail whipping wildly in the air. Trevor put the Jeep in reverse and gunned the pedal. The stinger struck down at them, grazing the hood as the vehicle sped backward.

Trevor pointed the vehicle toward the busted east gate and gunned it. The Jeep shook as it struck several arachnids along the way. As they reached the gate, Rob armed another block of C4 and tossed it out the window. Five seconds later, the explosive expanded into a vast ball of orange flame. A shockwave plowed through the front lawn, driving the horde into a frenzy.

The Empress raised her claws, enraged. She scampered forward and smashed into the maintenance shed, effortlessly ripping it to shreds. In moments, the structure had flattened.

The Empress turned and darted to the building, her drones quickly making way for her. She peered in through the breach and gazed upon the feeding frenzy taking place within. Scorpions backed away from the ravaged corpse, their jaws and pincers smothered in blood. She shrieked again, causing the drones to scurry out of the room. She reached in with one of her arms and snatched what remained of Muddler's corpse.

After gorging herself, she returned to the gaping hole she had created in the building. She entered the lobby and curved her body downward, slipping into the tunnel. She crawled deep beneath the earth, ready to continue her hunt.

CHAPTER 24

Golden beams of light stretched horizontally as the morning sun began to peek over the horizon.

The engine clunked and spat as the Jeep sped down the dirt trail. Trevor kept the pedal to the metal, soaring between two endless lines of trees. This trail was much straighter and smoother than the interior trail, allowing for greater speed.

The scientists and two mercenaries caught their breath. At this speed, they would be arriving at the harbor in minutes. They were still encased in shadow due to the trees, though the night sky had transformed into a golden bliss.

"Now we know what became of the experiment," Trevor said.

"Like a queen ant," Steele said. "I thought those things sat on their asses and laid eggs all day!"

"Spider Wasp DNA," Jean reminded him. "She lays eggs in living hosts. But right now, she's just hungry. They all are."

"Well, they'll find plenty of food in each other," Rob said.

"Amen to that," Steele said. "Let's just get to that damned beach."

Despite their good pace, Trevor still wished it was possible to move faster. At this point, anything short of hyperspace felt too slow to him. He watched the trail and the trees, trying to allow the island's natural beauty to sooth his nerves. Branches covered in bright green leaves swayed in the morning breeze.

In the wall of green were black spots. Trevor blinked, thinking it was his imagination. The spots were moving.

A scorpion leapt from its crouched position. With no regard for its own safety, it landed directly in front of the Jeep.

"Shit!" Trevor shouted. The Jeep plowed straight into it, causing shell and yellow syrupy blood to splatter all over the windshield. The impact shifted the Jeep's direction, causing it to sideswipe several trees.

Fighting for control, Trevor eased on the brakes and jerked the wheel to the right, almost accidentally thrusting them into the other tree line.

A huge thud reverberated and the overtop indented inward. Rob leaned down, seeing the tips of a scorpion's legs sweeping over the edge of the window. Like the other, it had leapt down from the trees.

"My God! Can't we get a break!" Trevor shouted.

"Keep it going!" Rob ordered, realizing more would likely follow.

The scorpion dug its chela into the overtop and pulled. The latches snapped and the passenger section ripped free. Rob looked up, seeing the creature tossing the object away. As it started to reach down, he pointed his rifle up and fired. The scorpion lurched back and spun in place, covering the breach with its belly.

Trevor swerved, seeing another scorpion in his path, poised to attack. Again, he grazed several trees. The Jeep shook with the various impact, knocking the injured scorpion free. It hit the ground behind them and rolled, legs and tail thrashing.

Trevor operated the windshield wipers. Blood smeared over the glass but the view was clear enough for him to see. They had to be no further than two miles from the harbor. He just had to keep going.

A wall of black briefly obscured his view. The windshield imploded as the scorpion landed down on it. Claws immediately reached in, snapping at Trevor's arms. He screamed as one clamped down on his wrist, ripping through his cuff. Blood seeped from the edges as they cut into his skin.

Rob thrust his rifle into the creature's face and squeezed the trigger. The scorpion's body vibrated as it absorbed the spray, unclenching its claw and falling away.

The Jeep swerved as Trevor tried to regain control, blindly hitting another scorpion in the process. The group grabbed for anything they could as it fishtailed and teetered on its left wheels. On the trail, another scorpion found its way in the spiraling vehicle's path. Tremors of impact shook the Jeep. It flipped and rolled like a barrel in a raging river before smashing into the base of a tree.

The world seemed to spin as everyone regained their senses. The Jeep was on its left side, the engine crumpled against the tree trunk. Rob pushed the passenger door open and crawled up and out.

Behind him, Steele did the same thing. Blood trickled from his brow due to hitting his head against the window. He glanced back, seeing at least five scorpions moving in on them.

Rob stepped toward them on wobbly legs, then shouldered his rifle. The nearest scorpion sprawled its arms out and started to dart at him. An onslaught of rounds tore its head open. It kept coming, determined to get to the soft meat. Blobs of flesh ripped apart as more bullets entered the crevice in its shell. Finally, the arachnid succumbed to its injuries and fell on its belly.

Steele emptied his submachine gun into the next one. "Get them out!" he yelled to Rob.

Rob didn't have much choice. His last magazine was empty now, rendering the weapon useless. He moved around the Jeep until he was near the overtop. Trevor was struggling to climb out, with an injured hand to add to his list of injuries.

"Pop the latches," he said. There was a moment of silence, as Trevor wasn't sure what he meant. "Up top. Pop the black hatches."

"OH!" Trevor turned the latches and pushed the top free. It lifted out and fell into the dirt. Rob reached in, cut the seatbelt free with his knife, and pulled Trevor free.

Jean lifted herself out, her moves somewhat sluggish from being dazed. Rob grabbed her by the waist and helped lift her out the rest of the way.

"Don't mind me," he joked.

"Don't worry, I won't go all *Hashtag MeToo* on you," she retorted.

Steele reloaded his gun and unleashed several bursts into another arachnid.

"Let's go!" Rob called to him, taking Jean's MP5 and hurrying around Jeep to give assistance. He barely cleared around the back before another scorpion leapt down from the trees, landing just a yard away from him. Rob blasted the creature, the first of several rounds crunching uselessly against the thick shell on its back. Adjusting his aim, he hit it in the vulnerable area along its face, driving it backward.

Steele backtracked, with two scorpions scurrying toward him. One final burst of gunfire emptied his MP5. With no more magazines, he was forced to toss the weapon aside and draw his sidearm.

With her AK-47 in hand, Jean ran to Steele's side and opened fire at the two remaining beasts.

"Go! Run!" he yelled.

Rob could barely hear him over the combination of gunshots and bestial screeches. He continued hitting his target, until finally it rolled to its side, face reduced to globs of flesh. He stopped to place a final magazine into the weapon.

The 'dead' scorpion sprang back to life. Leaping from poised legs, it tackled Rob to the ground. Pincers tore at his vest, slicing through fabric and flesh. Its blood seeped down onto his chest, the one remaining eye staring him in the face. He struggled, unable to outmuscle the beast. He saw the head pull back, making way for the dripping stinger.

With all of his might, Rob shifted his weight, moving his head several inches to the left. The stinger struck down, striking dirt instead of flesh. It pulled back, ready to reattempt its sting. Venom accumulated at the tip, forming a round droplet that spilled onto Rob's chest. He gritted his teeth in pain as it pressed its claws deeper into his chest, pinning him down firmly this time.

"Fuck YOU!" Steele shouted. The mercenary discarded his empty pistol and charged the arachnid, drawing his knife and machete. Like a tribal warrior, he threw himself on its back. The scorpion rolled to the side, freeing Rob from its grip.

The beast corrected its posture and bucked, throwing Steele off of its back. He hit the ground on his stomach, still gripping the weapons. He pushed up onto his knees as the scorpion came at him. The tail vaulted, its stinger aimed at his center.

Steele swung the machete, cracking the barb with his blade. The impact knocked the stinger to the side, causing it to miss entirely. The scorpion continued its advance. Claws stretched toward him and clenched his thighs. Steele yelled and fell backward, feeling the edges cut into his flesh.

Bleeding from his shoulders, Rob got off the ground and drew his pistol. The creature's back faced him, forcing him to move in a counterclockwise motion to be able to shoot its vulnerable face.

Pistol shots from Trevor drew his attention. Another creature had emerged from the trees and was coming directly at him. The scientist yelled, stumbling back as the creature neared him.

Rob ran at the creature, firing several rounds into it. It stopped its assault, now on the defensive. Its sensory organs detected the injuries in its head, forcing it to stumble back, as it couldn't comprehend the seemingly invisible projectiles that entered its body.

Steele cursed and swung the blade, again striking the stinger. This time the barb split wide open, spilling blood and venom onto the scorpion's back.

"My turn!" he yelled. He thrust the machete forward, plunging it deep through the fragmented shell in the creature's face. As the blade sunk all the way to the hilt, he raised his tactical knife high, then drove it down, stabbing the scorpion through its remaining eye.

The arachnid writhed in agony, then finally slumped on the ground, blood spurting from its head. The claws loosened, allowing Steele to back out of their grip.

The mercenary sucked in a quick breath, ignoring the pain from the lacerations in his thighs. He spun on his heel to assist the others.

The canvas exploded above him as another scorpion dove down. It struck several low-hanging branches on its way down, scattering leaves in a vivid display, before crashing down on Steele. Ribs crunched inwards as its weight plowed onto his body, forcing him down. Steele yelled in immense pain, spitting blood from his lips.

Claws immediately raked his shoulders and chest, exposing blood and bone. Steele shrieked and twisted. He swung the machete, striking the creature repeatedly in the face. After bouncing off its shell, the blade finally found one of its eyes. The eyeball decompressed, shooting blood mixed with watery fluid.

Steele tried swinging again, only to feel his forearms snapped after one of the pincers closed down on it. Steele yelled again, this time stabbing with his smaller knife. The blade struck the creature's shoulder and snapped, leaving the mercenary with a useless handle. The arachnid drove its claws into his chest, holding him down firmly.

Steele spat and cursed, the words coming out like rapid fire.

"Fuck you, you piece of shit! I hope a giant bird plucks your ass and swallows ya!"

The tail came down. The stinger punched straight through his right eye, bursting the eye socket inward until it entered his brain.

Rob emptied his magazine, finishing off the attacking scorpion just in time to see Steele receive his fatal blow. Anger coursed through his veins as the scorpion scuttled backwards into the woods, dragging a limp Steele in tow.

"He's dead," Jean said, sensing Rob's temptation to chase it. "I'm sorry, Rob. You can't help him." Of course, he already knew that. It was vengeance that fueled his desires. But the scientist was right. Steele was gone. Only *he* remained now. Only *he* could finish the mission.

"Let's go! We're not far from the beach," he said.

"Okay," Jean said. She tossed the AK-47 aside, having used up its last remaining magazine. They were down to pistols at this point. "Hope we'll last while we're there."

"There's weapons up there that we can use," Rob said. "Rifles and plenty of ammo. Even explosives, I think."

"Let's hope so," Jean said.

"I don't know if I can make it," Trevor said, clutching his leg.

"You're GOING to," Rob said. His authoritative voice snapped Trevor out of his brief moment of self-pity.

"Yes sir," he said, like a soldier answering a commander. The three survivors stuck together and raced east as fast as they could, carefully watching the trees in case of any new surprises.

CHAPTER 25

The sand beach glistened in the morning sun as the group arrived at the harbor. Trevor fell to his knees, completely out of breath and soaked in sweat. Jean kneeled next to him, equally out of breath.

"Damn, I need to start up jogging again," she muttered to herself. She closed her eyes and took in the breeze that came off the rippling ocean.

Only Rob remained on his feet. He dug through his side pockets and pulled out some gauze and medical tape, then reached through the slashes in his vest and shirt to cover his lacerations. A stitch job would definitely be required, but this would have to do for now.

Jean watched as he marched to the guard shack. He moved around to the front and entered through the busted doorway. Then came the sound of the metallic clunking of weapons being loaded up.

The man has a point, she thought. She stood up and hurried to the shack, while Trevor limped around behind it. The sight of the damage eliminated the feeling of sanctuary, as he realized he was looking at the aftermath of the scorpions' attack on the Cobras.

"Shit," he said. He found a rifle and used it as a crutch, while picking up a submachine gun with his other hand. He inspected the gun to see if it worked the same as the pistol. The magazine came out in a similar way. He put it back in and saw that the safety was already switched off. The only thing he wasn't sure about was the cocking lever, which was already pulled back.

"Careful with that." Rob's voice made him jump. Trevor looked to the window where Rob glared at him and held up the weapon. "Yep, that's how it's supposed to be. Magazine's probably only partly full. When you reload it, you'll have to cock that lever back."

"Gotchya," Trevor said. Rob turned away and continued rummaging through the armory, stocking grenades and ammo. Trevor continued exploring the beach, seeing several more weapons in the sand. He gazed down at an assault rifle. Its muzzle was buried in the beach, the frame covered in dry blood. He kept walking, noticing something else partly buried in the beach. It was far larger than any gun. He checked it out and brushed off the sand, exposing black rubber tires and a leather seat. It was a dirt bike.

The right handle was bent as well as the main shaft, which had a large groove down the side. The seat had been slashed and the gauges tattered. However, it seemed to be in functional condition.

Rob placed his newly acquired AKM down and reloaded another one while Jean looked at grenades and other weapons. After placing several full magazines in his vest, he discovered a thick case. A triumphant smile appeared on his face as he looked inside.

"This might come in handy," he said. Jean looked over, seeing him lifting an RPG out of the case.

"Excellent," she said.

They stood silent, hearing a faint droning sound. Engines!

"Hey!" Trevor yelled. They stepped out, seeing him pointing to the south.

The C-130 was about a mile out and was beginning its descent. The aquatic aircraft touched down along the water, its hull glowing a bright silver as it reflected the sun's rays.

Water rolled onto the shore as the plane traveled parallel to the shore, keeping about a hundred yards out. It came to a stop directly ahead of the busted dock. The ramp doors came down and two large zodiacs plunged into the water.

"Finally," Trevor said. Rob kept an eye out for the scorpions, aware that they weren't out of trouble until they got aboard that plane. The survivors assembled on the dock as the Zodiacs moved in. Rob counted as least four armed soldiers in each one, with Jayson riding in the front.

Jayson waved, sporting a rare smile as they approached.

Of course he was, Rob thought, *after all, I probably just elevated his career by eliminating a dangerous loose end.*

The smile faded, replaced by a confused scowl.

"You the only survivors?"

"Yes," Rob answered.

"Dr. Bischoff?"

"Dead. Killed by the experiments," Jean said bluntly.

"I see," Jayson said. There was no compassion in his voice. If anything, the bastard seemed relieved. Less people to worry about spreading the word, most likely. He faked a smile, as well as his gratitude. "You did well, Mr. Cashen."

"Listen, we can talk on the plane," Rob said. "Those things could arrive at any moment."

"How many of them are there?" Jayson asked. He sounded genuinely concerned this time.

"Too many," Rob said. "They killed my entire team."

Jayson looked like he was starting to sweat. He had planned for a cleanup crew to take over and eliminate the evidence. But if there was a swarm of mutations on the island, they would undoubtedly be slaughtered, and thus leave more evidence. After all, this island would likely be visited by someone at some point or another.

"They'll likely destroy each other within the next week," Rob said. Jayson glanced his way, his eyes hopeful.

"You believe so?"

"Oh yes, they have no qualms about devouring their own kind. They've eaten everything else on this island," Jean explained.

"That said, you mind pulling up closer so we can get out of here?" Rob shouted, his tone stern.

"Where is he?" Jayson said.

"Who?" Rob said.

"Isagana, of course," Jayson said.

"Listen, you prick! We're wasting time!" Rob snarled. His hands gripped tightly around the assault rifle. If he had to, he would gladly eliminate all eight of Jayson's soldiers and take their boats. AND their plane. He could smell a double-cross brewing in the air.

Never trust a government official.

"Where. Is. He?" Jayson said. His voice was calm and emotionless. He was safe in the water after all. The whole swarm could be crawling over the beach and it wouldn't affect him.

"He's dead," Rob said. "Just as you'd hired me to do. Back in the lake chasm where the bridge is...was...we had to blow it up."

"You were supposed to provide evidence," Jayson said. Rob said no.

"You do see me and my fiancée standing here, right?" Trevor said. "That ought to be proof enough that he did his job."

"Shut up," Jayson said. Cocking mechanisms slid back and the soldiers shouldered their guns. Trevor gulped but held his ground, as well as keeping his hand on the submachine gun he found.

Rob exhaled slowly through his nostrils. *It was never about rescuing hostages. It was only about killing Isagana and destroying any evidence.* He should've seen this coming.

Rob counted the soldiers again as well as the guns they carried. They were only a couple of feet away from each other. Only a couple had their rifles pointed and they were still pointed at Trevor. In addition, their fingers were still over the trigger guards. He could easily take out Jayson's boat in an instant.

The second group would be the main challenge. They had circled about a hundred feet out and were still in motion. The RPG might come in handy for that, if he hadn't left it near the shack.

The water swished as the hull passed over it. Tiny waves rippled out toward shore. They moved in a direct path, cresting and rolling again. That direct path turned into an arc. Rob found himself staring.

He felt another rumbling under his feet. A chill crept down his spine. Jean and Trevor felt it too, the latter glancing nervously at the ground. Jayson scowled, uncertain what had their attention.

"Sir?" someone from the other boat called out.

The water was now twisting like a merry-go-round. The water indented into a small crater and spun intensely.

"What the hell?" Jayson muttered in amazement. His stomach tightened as the realization struck that a massive whirlpool had just formed. The tide pulled back as the water began to fall into the earth, dragging their boat along with it. Even the plane was caught in the current. The wings tilted back and forth as though the aircraft was teetering on a fulcrum.

The soldiers of the second Zodiac started the engine. The propellers kicked up water as it pushed against the current. Little by little, it gained momentum.

There was another rumbling from below, followed by a deep grinding sound. Just then, the whirlpool slowed to a stop. The plane rocked back and forth as it drifted. The pilots inside panicked and started the engine as they realized they were heading right into the cargo ship. The turbines hummed loudly and the plane began to move.

"Get this thing back to shore," Jayson ordered his men.

"What's that?" one of the soldiers said. He was pointing back toward the plane. Jayson looked, freezing in fear as he watched the water churning under the nose of the plane.

The Empress rose like a vengeful demon. Huge pincers stretched high into the air then slashed down like butcher knifes into the nose of the C-130. The plane tilted forward as the beast pulled herself up onto it. Her tail lashed into the windshield, exploding the glass into the cockpit.

"Oh, SHIT!" Trevor yelled. He grabbed Jean by the arm and started pulling her back to the beach.

On the boat, Jayson watched in horror as the enormous scorpion dug its claws into the thick hull of the C-130. It reached inside and snapped its pincers onto the midsection of one of the pilots.

His screams echoed across the beachside as the Empress pulled him free from the cockpit. It held him high like a toy airplane, letting his blood drip into the water. The pincers tightened until the edges met. The pilot's two halves fell away and plunged into the reddening water.

The Empress snatched the pieces and placed them through her jaws. Still slurping entrails, she proceeded to ravage the plane. The co-pilot had moved into the fuselage. The beast watched through the windows, seeing the tiny creature's movements.

The rumblings from the engines drew her attention. Her brain registered the sound as a threat, a possible sign of aggression from this metallic behemoth. Those claws ripped into the nearest engine. Pieces of shrapnel exploded from the spinning motor, which then burst into flames. The Empress reeled upward and turned away, repelled by the heat. It turned and splashed down, wigging its segmented tail like an eel.

Automatic rifles rattled from the four soldiers in the Zodiac. They stood at the stern, emptying their magazines in an eighteen-second spray. The creature turned to the left, flickering its tail like a caudal fin. Curved spikes along its back sliced the water like dorsal fins. The soldiers reloaded and continued blasting away, their bullets smashing uselessly against her hide.

Realizing their guns were having no effect, the commanding officer on board turned and grabbed the helm. As his palm pressed against the throttle, the creature struck.

The boat flipped, sending all four men crashing into the waves. The Empress lifted the empty boat, stinging it with her tail, and slashing it with her claws until it broke in half. She snatched a metal fragment and fed it into her jaws, only to spit it out after discovering it was inedible.

It saw splashing in the water ahead of it. Four bite-sized creatures thrashed in the water, each fighting to keep their heads above the surface. Their gear weighed on them like cement blocks. Saltwater stung their eyes as they kicked their feet, fighting against the dead weight.

The Empress shrieked and drove its claws down. It raised them up, generating an enormous splash. The water rained back down, now red with the blood of the two soldiers that were diced in the pincers. Strung-out entrails floated along the wavy surface as the bodies were slurped into the Empress' gullet.

She gazed at the other two, who screamed as they tried swimming toward the shore. Neither of them completed a full stroke before the claws clamped down on them.

"Christ!" Jayson yelled, watching the carnage. The scorpion lifted her arms, holding the fleshy prizes high. Legs kicked as the victims dangled in her grasp. One of them literally dangled from the neck down, as the pincer had clamped down on his head. His screams were muffled, his skull slowly cracking as he was lifted toward her jaws. She tilted her head up and held him high like a cracker. The pincers clenched tighter, imploding his skull and peeling it away, allowing his twitching body to fall into the clamping jaws.

Still chewing the fresh victim, she brought the other one to her mouth. The soldier kicked and writhed, succeeding only in allowing the claws to squeeze tighter. Ribs snapped and his flesh was crushed down to his spine, driving his blood out through his mouth and anus.

The jaws clamped down on him, shredding him to bits as they tapped together with the speed of piranha jaws.

Behind it, the plane continued to burn. The fire spread into the interior of the wing, igniting the fuel tank precisely as the plane sank below the waves. The gasoline erupted like an underwater volcano, blasting up through the surface. The vibration and shockwave caused the Empress to lurch forward. She lashed out at the invisible attacker, striking nothing but smoke.

Unable to endure the heat, she quickly turned around and moved toward shore.

Jayson and his men backed away from their beached Zodiac toward the tree line.

Rob moved away from their group, knowing that the beast would be more interested in larger numbers. He stepped to the guard shack, his mind fixed on getting to that RPG.

Water sprayed as the Empress emerged thirty feet from shore. Her tail whipped like that of a dinosaur, shattering the extended portion of the dock. Jayson panicked and ducked behind his men.

"Kill it! Kill it! Kill AHHH!"

Claws tore through his jacket and into his back, dragging him backward. All eyes glanced back, seeing over a dozen scorpion drones joining the fray.

Another one grabbed Jayson by the legs and pulled against the other as though in a game of tug-of-war. The men converged, guns blazing.

The arachnids released their grip, driven back by the multiple impacts against their shell. Their hides cracked and split, opening them up like eggs.

The others spread out, with several of them flanking the soldiers. Two men grabbed Jayson by his collar and pulled him away, backtracking toward the beach...

...where the Empress was coming ashore.

Several yards down the beach, Trevor and Jean watched as the giant scorpion crawled onto the sandy beach. The soldiers realized their predicament and branched out.

The huge tail, at least twenty-feet in length, waved in the air like a tentacle. With no warning, it whipped down, plunging its stinger between the shoulder blades of a fleeing soldier.

The soldiers released their grip on Jayson and ran. It was every man for himself at this point. The nerves in his ankle flared, causing him to fall back to the ground.

The tail retracted, lifting its victim high over the ground like a giant shish kabab. The soldier was still alive, his body quickly going rigid as the venom took hold.

Jean watched as the tail pulsed.

"That's how she does it," Jean said. "She's laying her eggs."

"Well, I'm glad you're fascinated," Trevor said. The drones were spreading out, with three coming their way. He moved up the beach and grabbed the handlebars of the dirt bike. He ignited the engine then waved for Jean to follow him. "I'm not staying to have the same done to me!" She hopped on the bike and hugged her arms around his waist. Trevor gunned the bike, zagging between the arachnids toward the shack.

Rob saw a drone coming at him, pincers wide open. He pointed his AKM rifle and placed several rounds in its face, killing it. Trevor brought the bike around behind him.

"Come on, man!" Trevor yelled.

Rob shook his head.

"How do you expect me to fit on that?"

"I don't know, just figure out a..." Trevor's words were interrupted by the screams of one of the Filipino soldiers as four drones converged on him. His rifle had run dry, and in the rush of adrenaline he continued squeezing the trigger before realizing he had to reload. By then it was too late.

The arachnids lunged at once, pulling at his arms and legs, while others dug into his belly. Stingers struck and mandibles tore at flesh.

Rob could see others starting to emerge from the trees.

"Get out of here! Move up the hill!" he shouted.

"But Rob..." Jean said.

Another soldier screamed as the Empress lunged. Both claws lashed out, one grabbing him by the head, the other by his waist. An effortless tug pulled his head free of his neck.

The last remaining soldier backed away, emptying his assault rifle into a drone. Its dead body slumped down, only to be crawled over by its many brethren.

The soldier's breathing intensified. His eyes went over to the waterline, where the Zodiac remained...untouched. He took off in a mad dash, hoping to get around the gigantic Empress before she noticed his presence.

The twenty-foot tail lashed to the side like a whip. The soldier's dying grunt lasted a mere second as his body hurtled to the air, breaking apart at the waist.

"GO!"

Trevor accelerated the bike, kicking up sand as he weaved around the scorpions.

The Empress took notice of the small vehicle and the two soft-meat prey that rode atop of it. It moved in, lunging with its claws.

"Oh, hell no," Rob said. He snatched up the RPG and propped it over his shoulder. "Bite on this!"

The explosive projectile expelled from the barrel and struck the Empress on the left side, just above one of her legs. The explosion drove her down, rolling her to her right.

Rob took a moment to make sure the scientists made it to the base of the hill. They rolled up the gravel incline, successfully putting distance between themselves and the horde.

His eyes went back to the Empress. To his amazement, she was still alive.

"Damn bitch," he whispered. Her shell was cracked where the RPG struck, but still held together firmly. Her screams sent the horde into a frenzy. They rushed the beach, determined to protect their ruler.

Jayson was still on his stomach, attempting to crawl away from the leviathan. He froze, feeling the vibration of several advancing monsters crowding around him. He screamed as their shadows encompassed him. It made no difference that he wasn't the one that injured the Empress.

She had called out, and *he* was the closest in proximity, making him the likely perpetrator.

They drove their stingers down again and again. Jayson twitched and gurgled. He laid on his stomach, paralyzed, yet awake. He could see, hear, and feel. He could see their black bodies scurrying around him, claws extending. He heard the tearing of fabric. And he could feel the slicing of pointed claws punching through his spinal column as the creatures dug in.

Rob placed another round in the RPG launcher. Five of the creatures were grouped around Jayson. Flesh and blood were tossed in the air like confetti as they tore him apart.

Rob pointed the RPG at the tight grouping and fired. The round struck right in the middle of the group, blowing all five of the scorpions into bloody chunks.

"Bullseye," he said to himself.

The Empress shrieked again and rolled her body back onto its feet. Answering her call directly, more scorpions scurried out from the tree line. Rob exhaled sharply in frustration.

"You've got to be kidding me," he complained, seeing all of the creatures moving in toward him. The Empress continued walking inland until she arrived at the base of the hill. She would leave the drones to handle Rob, as she was more interested in the prey that had escaped her grasp moments before.

Rob fired his rifle, putting rounds in numerous bugs with precision. He counted his rounds, taking at least nine to successfully put down each creature. He reloaded after killing three of them and continued the defense. More bugs fell dead in a pool of their own blood. But the horde continued to draw closer.

He realized they would be all over him in seconds. Rob dove into the shack through the broken window. The scorpions immediately began tearing into the wall. Ribbons of steel peeled off like onion slices as they ripped into the structure.

Rob rummaged through the armory, finding several blocks of C4. He wired the explosives one-by-one, placing them over a box of grenades and RPG ammo.

"Here's your buffet, hot and ready," Rob said. He set the timer for ten seconds, then dashed through the building. He dove through the window on the south side, bursting the glass, and landing on his back. He sprung to his feet and leapt backward, narrowly dodging the snapping arms of one of the scorpions. He ran as fast as he could, making several yards before the shack exploded into a huge ball of shrapnel and flame. The shockwave hit Rob like a train, driving him to the ground.

Bits of scorpion rained down around him, scorched in hot fire. Claws, feet, shell, even a few stingers peppered the beach.

Rob sat up. His whole body ached. His ears were ringing, his wounds reopened, and much of his exposed skin was blackened with smoke. But the drones were dead.

He stood on wobbly legs and gazed up the hill. The Empress was near the construction site, eagerly pursuing Trevor and Jean.

"God damn, I'm too old for this shit," he said. He picked up his RPG launcher and spare round and sprinted for the hill.

CHAPTER 26

The wind whipped Jean's hair into a wild frenzy as Trevor drove the bike uphill. The horizon had turned back as the C-130's fuel burned on the ocean's surface. The air smelled of hot oil and salt, even as they elevated to the construction site.

She could feel vibrations under the bike. At first, she though it was just from the slightly uneven pavement. Then came the sounds of pounding and scraping behind her, causing her to glance back.

The Empress scampered up the pathway. Blood dripped from its breached hide, forming a yellow river behind it.

"Trevor!" she yelled. Her fiancé looked back.

"Does that bitch ever quit?!" he shouted. Jean gripped the MP5 and aimed it back as best she could. The endless shaking of the bike made aiming impossible. Bullets sprayed all over the place, with only a few striking the creature. The Empress didn't even feel the nine-millimeter bullets bounce off her skull. She kept coming, an unstoppable force hell bent on tearing her victims apart.

Jean let the weapon hang from its sling. She grabbed one of the grenades she took from the shack and bit the pin free with her teeth. She rolled the grenade behind her and ducked forward against Trevor's back. The Empress charged, ready to close the distance on her prey. The grenade burst from under her, causing her front legs to sprawl out. The beast let out an enraged roar as she fell onto her stomach, giving Trevor and Jean enough time to reach the top of the hill.

Trevor cursed as the tires struck several deep grooves within the trail. The bike rocked uncontrollably. He fought for control, only to accidentally angle the front tire directly into one of the deep grooves in the pavement. The bike flipped, throwing both occupants onto the dirt.

Jean groaned, his ribs and thighs bruised. She looked at their surroundings, seeing the ravaged trailers, and battered bulldozer. The Empress was coming their way. They could not outrun it. Nor could they hide in the trailers, which had been already torn apart. Judging by the battered condition of the bulldozer, hiding in the other construction vehicles would be equally futile.

She looked up at the radio tower. It was over sixty feet high, with a ladder leading all the way up to its antenna.

"Come on!" she yelled, grabbing Trevor by the back of his shirt. He groaned, his leg throbbing. He could imagine the bullet fragments scraping against his muscle tissue with each step. Despite this, he praised the morphine, as without it, he would likely not even be able to stand at this point.

They grabbed the ladder bars and climbed as fast as they could. The beast emerged at the edge of the hillside and quickly darted across the construction site, shredding the ground with its feet.

Trevor reached high with each grab, clearing three bars at a time. He glanced down as he went to make sure Jean was right behind him. In seconds they were halfway up.

The Empress smashed the trailer, sending scraps of metal sheet raining into the trees. Finally, she turned, seeing the meat ascending up the strange artificial structure. They were out of reach, even from that of her tail. She struck anyway, the stinger landing less than a foot shy of Jean's shoes.

She yelped at the resulting *clang*. There was no pain, nor any other sign of injury. Not bothering to look back, she kept climbing.

The Empress hissed, lashing again at the tower. Her enormous claws clamped onto the foot of the tower. She pulled her body close to it as though in an embrace. Her four front legs reached up and took hold. All at once, they lifted her body up.

Now Jean could feel the reverberation within the metal structure as well as the shift in weight. This time she looked down, immediately seeing those enormous eyes staring back at her. The creature climbed further up, moving several feet in a single step.

Those deadly pincers opened and reached toward her.

Frozen by terror, Jean let out a horrified scream.

"Too old," Rob muttered through gritted teeth as he sprinted up the hill. His knees popped and his thighs burned. Sweat stung his eyes, fogging his glasses. He tore them off and tossed them aside.

He could hear Jean's screams, followed by a carnivorous snarl.

The top of the hill was just a hundred yards away. Rob charged as fast as he could, arriving at the top in under a count of ten. He immediately saw the Empress climbing up onto the tower, its claws extending toward the scientists. The structure began tilting toward the jungle, slowly succumbing to her weight.

"Hey, you fat bitch," he said. To his slight surprise, the creature stopped, then turned her big ugly head in his direction. *Seems the female of every species objects to weight remarks.* Rob pointed the RPG. He held his breath to steady his exhausted body, then fired. The rocket struck under her right arm. The beast screamed as the explosion launched her backwards, causing her to roll into the trees. Fragments of shell rained down around the tower, trailing globs of blood. The tail whipped aimlessly and the legs frolicked until the beast righted herself.

Rob stood in disbelief. That bitch had taken two RPG rounds but was still alive.

"Unbelievable," he groaned. The beast scampered away from the tower, moving behind the now-flattened trailers until coming around to the paved runway. He watched as those eyes locked on to him. The pincers clamped, letting his mind envision what his final upcoming moments would be like.

"Yeah, I bet you wanna butcher me worse than a *Disney* remake," he muttered. The creature shrieked as though in direct response.

Rob's brain went to work on a tactical solution. He had no more rockets for the launcher. Bullets would be useless against it. All he had were grenades, which also had proven ineffective even when exploding at point blank range. However, with the shell now weakened, a well-placed grenade detonation *might* do the trick.

He had only one remaining. He grabbed it from his vest and reached for the pin.

With a trumpeting roar, the Empress charged.

"Oh, shit," Rob said. With no time for the grenade, he took off in a sprint. Knowing he wouldn't get far running. Directly ahead was the backhoe, its platform door ajar. He could hear the beast closing in behind him. He could imagine its claws bearing down on him.

He reached the backhoe and propped his hands on the tracks, losing the grenade as he pushed himself up onto the platform. The pounding arachnid's footsteps came to a halt. It was right behind him. Rob yanked the door open and dove inside. Glass immediately shattered as the claws assaulted the cockpit. The frame supports buckled and the top crumpled inward like an empty soda can.

Rob glanced back, seeing the tail coiling behind the Empress' shoulder. He crouched low. The stinger struck, hitting the back of the cab. It retracted, then struck again, this time striking through the window. The barb passed inches above Rob's waist and struck the leather seat. Dripping venom, the tail recoiled again, only to be stuck in the window frame. The Empress tugged back, unable to pry her appendage from its entrapment. The backhoe rocked violently, shaking the occupant inside.

Rob looked up at the controls. The keys were still in the ignition. He knew outrunning the creature would be impossible, leaving one other option: fight it.

He turned the key. The engine roared to life. The internal computer system came on. The screen flashed blue with the word *Loading...* stagnant in the center.

"Oh, you've got to be kidding me..." Rob muttered.

The Empress gave a final tug. The tail snapped free, ripping out a ribbon of steel. The creature poised, gazing through the enlarged opening with its two enormous eyes. It raised its pincers and reached for the cockpit.

A barrage of gunshots struck its shell. Fifty feet up in the air, Jean and Trevor fired bursts from their MP5s. The Empress didn't even notice them at first, as the bullets were stopped cold against her back. They focused their aim on the cracked area near her right arm and unloaded into it. Bullets ricocheted off the fractured shell, gradually chipping away at it. Finally, a few of them punched through.

The Empress turned, its nerves detecting new damage. It backed away and turned toward the sound.

Rob propped himself up onto the seat and saw the Empress screeching at the tower. She was mad and hungry at once; the worst combination.

The computer beeped. *Starting...*

"Finally," he muttered. He released the parking brake and depressed the service brake pedal. He grabbed the computer-style joysticks at the helm. The one on the left moved the boom and swung the entire backhoe side to side, while the one on the right moved the stick and the bucket. Rob floored the accelerator and raised the arm high, plowing the vehicle hard into the Empress.

The arachnid crab-walked to the side, shrieking at the fourteen-thousand pound metal behemoth that dared challenge her. Rob pressed the assault and closed in, keeping the arm angled off to the right. As he expected, the Empress moved in and reached with both arms. He swung the boom across, knocking the left arm behind the elbow. The Empress stumbled off balance, exposing her weakened area near her back legs.

Rob seized the opportunity and brought the bucket down vertically. The forks plowed into the weakened shell, causing blood to spout as though he struck oil.

The Empress writhed. Segmented legs flailed and the tail whipped. Rob kept the pressure down on her, keeping her from rolling out of his grip. Her body ached backward as she twisted and pulled. A chunk of shell fell off her body as she broke away from the deathly grip. Not a moment had passed before she threw herself onto the vehicle.

The cab shook and the gears groaned as the Empress clamped down with her claws and pushed. Rob rocked hard in his seat as the backhoe was forced backwards. He brought the arm down on her back then raked the bucket along. Though it didn't breach the shell, it did block a sting. The Empress lurched, releasing her grip on the cab in favor of the boom. Rob tried swinging the backhoe, only to hear the gears groaning so loud he thought they would burst like pipes. The Empress attacked the hydraulics with her pincers, crunching metal with the razor edges.

Realizing she was no longer pushing back, Rob put the tracks in forward gear and gunned it. The backhoe rammed the scorpion like a bulldozer. The tracks hit her underbelly and the cab smashed against her face. Rob leaned back as best he could while keeping a grip on the controls. The frame caved in slowly, with the creature's face leaning in behind it. Pincer jaws clicked against metal. The tail lashed blindly, striking the arm. It struck again, this time arching low and skidding against the frame.

Rob continued pushing her back. He eyed the edge of the cliff behind her. With her shell weakened, a two-hundred foot fall down would splatter her onto the rocks.

Finally, the Empress managed to get her footing. She scuttled to the left, successfully getting out of the backhoe's way. Rob cursed and quickly tried putting it in reverse. In that instant, he saw a wall of black coming in toward the window. The Empress slammed her body hard against the Backhoe, crunching the cab inward.

Rob pulled on the joysticks, swinging the boom hard to the right, then raised the hydraulic as high as it could go. The boom struck the Empress in the head, rolling her slightly to her left side, leaving the fresh wound behind her right arm exposed. Rob brought the bucket down and stabbed the forks through the weak shell.

The Empress shrieked and thrashed her body. She barrel-rolled to the left, quickly freeing herself. She sprawled on all eight legs, now behind her enemy. Rob cursed, his maneuver having backfired. He drove the backhoe forward to put distance between himself and the beast. Suddenly, it doubled in speed as the Empress attacked from behind.

Rob rocked the joysticks to redirect the backhoe's direction, but could not free it of her grasp. He looked ahead, seeing the cliff drawing nearer.

"Shit," he said. He lifted his foot off of the accelerator.

The stinger struck the engine. Sparks streaked out like fireworks while grey smoke trailed high.

Rob muttered curses with each breath as he tried fighting for control. The scorpion continued her assault, bashing the cab with her claws. Rob ducked as the ceiling caved inward. Red lights flashed along the dashboard, indicating engine and hydraulic damage. He tried rotating the boom but could only turn so far. Something had jammed. He put it in reverse and hit the accelerator. The backhoe slammed against the Empress, enraging her further.

He rotated the boom a hundred-eighty-degrees in an attempt to swipe her away. It only made it about halfway before coming to a sudden stop. The Empress had clamped down on the hydraulics with her claws and pulled her body up onto the cab, jamming the gears with her immense weight.

Propped on top of the backhoe, she directed her assault on the thick steel holding the arm together. Razor claws closed over the cylinder and twisted. The mechanism crunched inward, jamming the dipper, which left the arm in a bent position.

Jean felt her heart thumping faster and faster as she watched the beast crush the backhoe. Bits of metal tore away as her claws laid waste to the cab. Rob could not shake her off, thus would be unable to escape. And retreating on foot would be certain death for him.

She couldn't sit by and do nothing. She glanced back to the bulldozer, which had been parked next to the backhoe.

"Hey! What the hell are you doing?!" Trevor yelled as she slid down the bars. She ran to the bulldozer and climbed in. She went to turn the ignition only to realize there was no key.

"Shit!" she yelled. She inspected the floor and seat but it was nowhere in sight. The damn fools probably stored it somewhere in the trailer, which was now completely ravaged. She stepped out and searched along the ground, hoping that by some miracle it had been dropped nearby during the chaos that had taken place before.

Her eyes locked onto the grenade that Rob had dropped earlier. Jean snatched it off the ground and placed a finger in the ring.

She glanced at the Empress, seeing the blood seeping in large rivers from her left hind quarters. She took a quick breath and ran until there was only about a hundred feet between her and it. She pulled the pin, waited a moment, then threw the grenade. It struck the Empress on her back side and bounced, exploding a few feet away from the wound. Blood and shell burst as the concussion shook the injured area. Shell peeled off, making way for a thick stream of blood.

The Empress fell backward and rolled, kicking her legs in the air. She cried out as the two legs nearest to the wound fell off completely, their joints having been worn down from the constant bombardment.

Rob sat in a hunched position. The ceiling pressed down against his head, the entire cab having been almost entirely crushed down on him. He could see the creature to the left, bleeding profusely. Praying for the engine to still be functional, he put the backhoe in reverse. Despite clunky gears, it moved. He steered it back to the left until he was lined up precisely with the creature.

She stood up, her jaws clamping repeatedly. She turned around and stared directly at her mechanical opponent.

Rob accelerated the backhoe at full speed. The two titans collided with a resounding *boom*. The Empress twisted, unable to push back with as much strength. Rob raised the boom and brought the bucket down on her head. With the arm stuck in its bent position, the claws came down directly on her neck, pinning her to the backhoe.

She roared in defiance, repeatedly striking the backhoe with her tail as it pushed her back.

Rob kept the pressure on the accelerator and watched the cliff edge. It was thirty feet away. Twenty-five. Twenty. He extracted his knife and thrust it down through the accelerator into the floor, pinning it down just enough to keep it going.

Rob kicked the side door, breaking it clean off.

"Adios," he yelled, then dove out onto the grass.

The backhoe kept pushing. The Empress shrieked. Her remaining hind legs pushed back to no avail. Suddenly, there was nothing to push off of.

For a moment she was weightless. She descended down the wall of the cliff, letting loose one final scream before hitting the rocks. Yellow blood filled the ocean as her shell split apart over the jagged edges.

Half-a-second later, the crane came down on top of her, sandwiching her figure with its fourteen thousand pounds of weight. Cracks spread from the ruptured areas across her body, splitting her down the middle. Her left eye exploded, sending an orange stream of fluid spilling into the water. Her tail twitched and convulsed, then slowly stiffened.

Jean and Trevor joined Rob at the cliff edge. Together, they gazed down at the dead titan.

Trevor broke the silence. "Any of you have a giant paper towel?" All three of them shared a laugh.

Jean looked further out to the ocean and watched the smoke swirling from the exploded C-130 Hercules. Pieces of wreckage bobbed in the water as they rode the tide to shore.

"I hate to be a buzzkill, but we've lost our ride. What the hell are we gonna do now?" she asked.

Rob pulled the satellite phone from his back pocket.

"I'm sure we can put this to good use," he said. A breeze brushed over them and rustled the trees. They cautiously watched the jungle, wondering how many scorpions might be lurking on the island. "But first, let's get down to that damn Zodiac. Don't know about you, but I've had my fill of fighting oversized bugs."

"I've had my fill of this island in general," Trevor said. He put his arm around Jean and hugged her close. "How 'bout a trip somewhere...I don't know...with snow?"

"I like skiing," she said, smiling. They embraced each other passionately.

"Oh, jeez," Rob said, mimicking disgust. "Just do me a favor and don't create any hybrid sasquatch monsters while you're there."

"You got it," Jean joked. They stepped away from the cliff and started their journey down the hillside. "So Rob? You like weddings?"

Rob smiled. "I'll be there. Just don't film me dancing."

"We'll make a note of it," Jean laughed.

THE END

HECK OUT OTHER GREAT
ORROR NOVELS

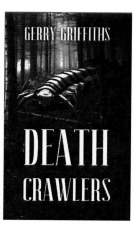

DEATH CRAWLERS
by Gerry Griffiths

Worldwide, there are thought to be 8,000 species of centipede, of which, only 3,000 have been scientifically recorded. The venom of Scolopendra gigantea—the largest of the arthropod genus found in the Amazon rainforest—is so potent that it is fatal to small animals and toxic to humans. But when a cargo plane departs the Amazon region and crashes inside a national park in the United States, much larger and deadlier creatures escape the wreckage to roam wild, reproducing at an astounding rate. Entomologist, Frank Travis solicits small town sheriff Wanda Rafferty's help and together they investigate the crash site. But as a rash of gruesome deaths befalls the townsfolk of Prospect, Frank and Wanda will soon discover how vicious and cunning these new breed of predators can be. Meanwhile, Jake and Nora Carver, and another backpacking couple, are venturing up into the mountainous terrain of the park. If only they knew their fun-filled weekend is about to become a living nightmare.

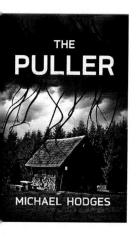

THE PULLER
by Michael Hodges

Matt Kearns has two choices: fight or hide. The creature in the orchard took the rest. Three days ago, he arrived at his favorite place in the world, a remote shack in Michigan's Upper Peninsula. The plan was to mourn his father's death and figure out his life. Now he's fighting for it. An invisible creature has him trapped. Every time Matt tries to flee, he's dragged backwards by an unseen force. Alone and with no hope of rescue, Matt must escape the Puller's reach. But how do you free yourself from something you cannot see?

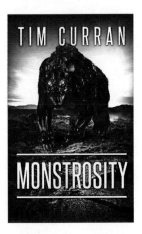
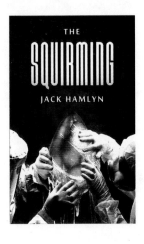

Made in United States
North Haven, CT
14 April 2025

67986472R00102